The Golden Horse

StarFields

Fairy Tales
For The Magical Child:

The Golden
Horse

By StarFields

Illustrations by Sheryl Tongue

DragonRising
Publishing UK

The Golden Horse
Bedtime Stories For The Angel Child
16 Original Fairy Tales For Magical Children Of All Ages
© StarFields 2000/2007

ISBN 187348397X
First Edition, First Printing

Published by
DragonRising Publishing
18 Marlow Avenue
Eastbourne
East Sussex BN22 8SJ
United Kingdom
www.DragonRising.com

Also By This Author:

   In Serein 1 – Sorcerer & Apprentice
   In Serein 2 – The Cage
   In Serein 3 – The Masterpiece

   Vampire Solstice

   The Magician

   Project Sanctuary

Sheryl thanks her models, Jakoby, Ty, Josh, and James
for their patience and good humor in posing for these pictures.

Dedicated To

Marion Bradley
Hans Christian Andersen
& Oscar Wilde

Thank you for your stories.

SFX 2005

Table of Contents

Elory's

Joy

Right here, right now, there exist many worlds and many foreign places. Amidst these worlds, some travel, and the most famous and renowned amongst these, are the story tellers.

It is their job and purpose to weave all these worlds together, as they take a tale or an occurrence from one world and they take it to the next, or another.

Here, they tell the tale and learn a fresh one, and so they move from world to world, and leave behind a silken thread of story and of information. Once such a thread has been created, the worlds are not alone any longer, for these fine first threads are channels, lines of communication, through which more and further stories and ideas then travel.

So the story tellers, they bind the universe and they are tradesmen, for it is often true that a story that is all too common on one world and deemed to be so ordinary, if told on another, will solve a puzzle of the ages, or be received just like the greatest and the shiniest of treasures.

But there are other worlds where evil lords and evil kings rule; and these do not want for the story tellers to come and bring their riches, bring their new ideas, their splendours or their tales of diamonds, sparkling beings that swim and dance in oceans of abundance, turquoise, light as light itself; for if the people who lived and suffered under their cruel treatment were to hear those stories, think about those things, they would begin to ask, "Why is our world so dour and so grey?"

For the evil lords in their stone towers, this would be disastrous; their reign and absolute dominion over the people who were nothing but their slaves would soon be broken and could never be repaired; and so on these worlds, it was very dangerous for a story teller to be seen or heard, and yet it was those very worlds that the bravest and the best of all the story tellers would seek to find, for they well knew the suffering of those who lived there, and they knew that just a single tale, a single well thought poem or a song could break that night in two and start a revolution, an evolution towards a very different state of being.

The story tellers knew full well that they were risking life and limb and all the many years they could have spent in comfort and delightful exploration, but they were very brave and very honest men and women from across the range of beings that resided on the many worlds, and in the star-filled voids that lay between them; from the dimensions that are other than we know or have experienced, for each and every race of beings send their very best to be a story teller and to help bring light and wide expansion where before, there was a prison made from stone and iron strong.

So the story tellers would sail their splendid ships across the endless seas of time and space and the dimensions, and they would look and seek and find another world, and they would bring their ships in orbit, matching the vibration and the resonance of that new world, and then they would begin to move into that world, re-shaping all they are so that they could then move amongst the beings there and look and seem the same as they.

At first, they would make sure to learn the stories of that world, for in the stories of the world there lies the essence of that world; an understanding of those beings and their aims and plans, their dreams and their desires, their flaws and their misunderstandings, as well as any ancient curses they might carry still.

And when they had the measure of the world and all its stories, they would then know which story there to tell; which story there to speak or write or sing or dance to the inhabitants, one that was the right one so that it would be remembered, taken gladly and passed on, from an elder to a youngster, from a youngster to a peer, and when the story had now fully taken hold, their work was done and they could leave, return to their proud ship, regain their shape of home and make their way to a new world, and on the way they would condense from all the stories they had learned a new one, one that would be added and now told again, so that the essence of that world was also now remembered and became a part of that most glorious web that they would spend a lifetime weaving, making wider, greater and still more profound.

But right at the heart of the web, in the very centre indeed, there lay a world that was the story teller's own.

And it was here that the story tellers would come for rest and relaxation; to meet their friends of old and to have festivals of joy and recognition.

Here too was a repository, a place where all the stories from all the worlds all the many story tellers had ever visited where brought together and shared and held, so that the story tellers did not just know the tales that they themselves had learned but all the stories that had ever been collected.

This was a most amazing place, a most holy place, of brilliant brightness for each story was a star of light and here, each one was placed within a many layered map that corresponded to the world from which it came, and so right here there was a true map of the living universe unfolding, being built a generation on the next, and getting brighter, getting more intense with every story added, and with every story teller who came home to add the treasures they had found, small stars of ruby, emerald, topaz, sapphire, amethyst and all the many colours of the planes and states of being to the universal map.

But more than light, each story was as well a song, and so the wondrous universal map did sing a chorus that was wonderful and strange, incredibly enlightening and healing too, and thus it was that not just story tellers visited here at the very centre of the web, but also many, many others — artists and healers, those who needed art or healing, lost ones, disenchanted ones and many, many others from around the worlds would come and be inside the universal map and leave, with a difference inside and out, having been most deeply re-aligned and stimulated by the colours and the feelings and the songs of all those many stories from across the times, the spaces and the manifold dimensions.

Wizards came, and scientists; farmers and engineers; beings of all kinds and many doing, thinking things we cannot know but all had questions, problems and conundrums of their own, and just being there inside the singing map of the known universe gave them an inspiration, maybe two or three, and even though the map did not exactly answer back when things were asked, it always helped them find new ways, try different things and generally, come back full of desire and of energy to return to their specific labours, tasks and works afresh and in a whole new way.

But there was also one more thing about the map.

It gave the bravest and the best of all the story tellers an idea just where to search for the forgotten worlds, the hidden worlds, the ones that sought to stay away and keep their people to themselves and in the darkness of their making, the ones that simply didn't know there was a web to join, and those who were all broken up inside for chaos or catastrophe.

The universal map of lights and sounds and all dimensions had a pattern, you see.

If you stood in the centre of the map and slowly turned around, there you would find some places, areas where you would know a light should be but it was missing; and as the map did correspond in shape and size to worlds and suns and stars, you could now take a craft and plot a course to take you there, right there where it was clear a world should be, but on the map, no star was shining softly, and there was no voice that told the tale or sang its song.

And on this day as we are here, we see a story teller and some say, this is the greatest of them all, a one called Elory from a race of beings that are rare, and old, and no-one knows quite where or when their homeworld was, a being smooth and radiant both of shifting shape, reflecting all the many colours and the lights as it observes the map around, above, below and searches for a dark world, for that is its speciality.

Elory doesn't search with eyes alone, or ears or any sense that would be known in such a way; it knows that soon enough, if it is still and most attentive, something will draw its attention towards it — a ripple in the flow, a missing shadow, a minute disruption in the song, those are the clues for which Elory searches and wide open in acceptance, lets its finely tuned awareness do the work.

A group of young apprentices from many worlds in robes of white that seem so multicoloured here within the map is standing to one side, most quiet they are and most reverend, for they are learning from Elory on this day just how it simply listens, draws the patterns of the song and sound within itself and they, young as they are, indeed are fortunate as they perceive a shift in the most ancient story teller's states of being.

Elory has found a dark world.

All eyes, all senses, feelers and receivers tune towards that part within the map and once this first and clear direction has been set, there is no question — it is obvious that here within the grid, there is a missing link, a place that isn't there but it must be, for else the pattern would not, could not work at all.

A most communal shiver of excitement, tinged with just a little fear goes through the beings who are here as all tune in and focus on that old, forgotten world, but then Elory's joy and bright begins to resonate, and touch them all, and makes them wonder, hope and pray that once the day will come when they will too be able and allowed to seek and find, perform the greatest and the hardest of all service and bring home a long forgotten world and all its beings to the web of all.

Elory leaves and sweeps away, full of its purpose and with great delight, so forward pointing, not a doubt, and this is learning now indeed for all the young ones as they know and understand, feel right inside themselves Elory's joy — how could it fail? With such conviction and the wisdom of the ages, this one dark world was saved already with Elory for a champion, just the instant that the ancient story teller had there heard its call and went to answer it forthwith.

And so, having learned this day what they did come to understand, the young apprentices are light and easy, and they take this opportunity to touch a star, to listen to a song and gain a story, maybe two, each one a gift and each one ready, waiting to inspire them and help them on their way.

The
Golden
Horse

Once upon a time, when the land was a little brighter and softer than it is today, there was a beautiful wild horse and it was golden and free.

Fast like a summer breeze, it would race across the soft green hills sloping gently to sun-sparkly lakes and to the blue hills in the distance, and in the sweet summer nights, it would sleep beneath the silver moon in a sky of darkest blue whilst the stars were smiling from above.

But there were people, and amongst them one, a dark man of grim countenance, who envied the horse its golden beauty and its riches, and his heart grew ever darker even as the children would point and laugh in delight and run and skip like horses do, their long curls and straight locks bouncing like the horse's tail in the wind.

So the dark man drew a dark plan, and one night, he set a devious trap for the golden horse made of flowers and the sweetest grass, and when the golden horse went to the offering he had prepared in the clearing by the fairy's brook, he entrapped it and ensnared it with ropes and with chains.

Oh, how the golden horse shrieked and fought! Oh, how the golden horse struggled against the chains and the ropes that were cutting deep into its silken flanks, and how it reared and kicked but all the time, the dark man just laughed for he had tied his end of the ropes and chains to a tree which grew straight into the earth and was stronger than the golden horse could ever be.

All through the night, the golden horse fought for its freedom.

All through the night, the stars watched with sadness and deepening compassion from high above as the golden horse grew weaker, and weaker still, yet it would keep fighting and struggling and would not lay down. Neither could the golden horse rest not even for a moment, for if it tried to stand and catch a breath, the dark man would whip the horse with a coarse and knotted whip, drawing bloody lines across its face and body, and forcing the golden horse to rear again and spend ever more of its precious power.

All through the day which dawned so sad and grey, and where the sun never showed her face behind the clouds, the golden horse fought and reared and struggled against the chain and whip and rope, and the children from the village came and saw, drawn by its cries they came and they cried too and begged the dark man to stop, but he just laughed and hit the horse the harder still and so the children fell silent and watched their hearts tearing with pain and there was nothing they could do and so they silently stole home and prayed so that they may be able to forget what they had seen and what they heard and what they had felt.

As the grey and weary day drew to a bloody dusk, the horse could no longer stand, and as the grey shadows merged into the mist of night, it sank to its knees and touched the beautiful golden face to the ground, and the dark man laughed and laughed and he rained blows upon it such as the world had never seen, but the horse neither cried nor moved nor struggled any more.

The dark man then went in the last of that terrible day's light and knelt before the horses face, Its eyes wore closed yet it woll knew him there, but it neither cried nor moved nor struggled any more as the dark man's hand fell heavily on its face and his voice fell heavily on its heart — "Now you are mine, to do with as I please. And don't forget, that I will be your master hereon in, and you will do my bidding in all ways."

The dark man rose and tied the horse's legs with stout rope, and into the horse's gentle mouth he placed a horror of rusted steel and tied it tight, and then he laughed again and walked off into the night with not a backward glance.

The horse lay by the fairies brook amidst the cold damp mist of the heartless night and neither cried nor moved nor struggled. In its heart and in its mind there was a pressure and a pain that was so great that all the hurts and cuts and bruises of its weary body were nothing, and the pressure and the pain was so great that the horse's heart would explode if it beat just one more time.

And at that moment, from the horse there rose a ghostly form, a white form of pure light, of pure radiant light and beauty, and it was a unicorn being born and released and rising fully from the fallen horse, it straightened and stretched, so pure and white if you but could have seen it, a mane of flowing silver and a flowing silver tail, shimmering in the darkness.

The unicorn rose and moved away from the dark shape of the beaten horse, unsure and wondering, pure in its new birth and not understanding, and then it raised its beautiful head towards where the moon was hiding still behind the darkest nightly clouds and leapt and like a flash, and was gone.

The beaten horse remained alone in darkness and though the pain was great, it slept and never dreamed, not even once.

In the morning, the dark man came with other men and other horses and they pushed and pulled and whipped until the golden horse would stand, then stumble on the road. And the golden horse which was no longer golden and not beautiful, all covered in mud and dirt and blood, was put into a grim stable where the stones were grey and lichen grew in the cracks and the hard ground was barely covered with mouldy straw and dreary dead things that once were grass was all there was to eat, and stale cold water hard and barely living was all there was to drink, and nothing to be seen of silken hills or sky or of the blue mountains or the stars.

In time, the wounds on the skin of the once golden horse healed, and in time, there were just scars on its legs and flank, and in time, the once golden horse no longer sighed when walking because its feet were so heavy with the iron they had nailed to them.

In time, the golden horse would drag its heavy loads to market, or the weary iron plough, or whatever the dark man decided, and in time, no-one seemed to remember what had been lost, and it was only the children in the village who would avert their eyes and never look at the horse that was just brown not golden, that was just plain not beautiful, and as time went by even they started to forget that they had ever known a different time at all.

There was one, though, who remembered.

It gave the dark man never ending pleasure to see what once had been the golden horse in front of heavy ploughs and carts and weights too much for its slim feet and slender neck, and he would often order the stable master to use what once had been the golden horse for tasks much better suited to another of the tired horses, and the stable master although old and not a one to give a thought or care, began to wonder why it was that the dark man rejoiced so in that horses sufferings.

Twenty years or more went by — who is to say? In all that time, the horse that once had been the golden horse never sighed anymore, never wept and when it slept, it never dreamed, not even once.

Far, far away from the village, in another space and time altogether, there lived a being of magic. This being was neither a man nor a woman, but something altogether different. It was neither child nor old, for it lived by a time which is altogether not like the one we know. It was neither dark nor light, but altogether of the colours that we only know when we are fast asleep and dreaming.

This being of magic lived in ways we cannot understand, and one day it was in its garden, thinking thoughts the like we have never known, and doing things the like of which we wouldn't understand, when it noticed a unicorn grazing amongst the flowers that grew there (flowers the likes of which you never saw nor even could imagine).

"Who are you?" asked the being, for it had been many a starfall and starbirth since a visitor had found their way to this place.

The unicorn looked up, surprised yet unafraid, for it sensed that the being of magic was an understanding one, and so it thought to find an expression that would serve to answer in a polite way, thus addressed.

"I do not know," the unicorn said at length.

"Why are you here?" asked the being.

"I do not know," the unicorn replied and shook its head so that silver bright mane flew like banners.

"What is your purpose?" asked the being of magic.

"I can't remember", said the unicorn, and sighed and then it started to cry softly, for sadness had befallen it, yet what it was it did not know or understand.

The being of magic understood that this unicorn was a lost soul, a one that wanders amidst the planes, never at home, never at rest, blowing like a leaf on the breeze. The being of magic understood that this unicorn was very sad, and it wove compassion in the way that only beings of magic can, a rainbow curtain of blue and green, like a soft and silken blanket it would lay across the unicorn, and the unicorn stood and let the blue and green soothe its sadness and its loneliness and it didn't feel quite so lost and sad deep down below.

The being of magic understood that the unicorn would need to find its purpose to truly heal the sadness within, and it called forth resolution as only a being of magic can, a whirlpool of whispering sounds that spun around and around and swept up the unicorn and took it to...

It was a bright summer's day, and a young boy and a young girl were sitting by the fairy brook. They were very sad because their mother and father had died, leaving them alone in the world and at the mercy of an old aunt, who neither cared to feed them nor to listen to their voices.

They were much alike, for they were twins and in spite of their sadness, they were glad of each other's comfort and company, and being here by the fairy brook where all was quiet and peaceful together soothed their hearts, so they came here often and they would talk about their mother and their father and their loss.

This day, they had come and they had done their talking, and their holding of hands, and just sat and listened to the sounds of the brook, and the rustling of the wind in the trees beyond, and the buzzing of the small flying things, and the warmth of the sun on their heads and shoulders, and the cool wet of the grass beneath, and letting their thoughts drift with the fluffy white clouds above, when they heard a whirlpool of whispering, a strange sound like they had never heard before.

And on the other side of the brook, as the sounds began to fade away, a ghostlike shape appeared, and it looked like something their mother had shown them in the old leather bound book she had kept high up on the kitchen shelf and as one, they remembered and they said its designation, "Unicorn" in hushed tones as not to frighten the creature that had appeared before them.

The unicorn looked directly at them, and saw them, and it spoke, with a voice like gentle bells, "You can see me."

And the children nodded carefully, as not to frighten it away and the little girl said, "You are a unicorn".

The unicorn lowered its beautiful head with a shell shiny horn that shone like newest silver in the sun.

"I am lost," said the unicorn. "I need to find my way home but I cannot. Will you help me?"

The boy and the girl looked at each other, and the boy said, "We are lost also, and we have no home also. How can such as us be of help to one like you?"

The unicorn sighed deeply and made as if to turn and walk away, and the little girl sprang to her feet. "Please don't go!" she cried, and the unicorn stopped and turned its head towards her questioningly.

"It is true we are lost and have no home, but perhaps together we can find a way? Perhaps we can do something if we just think, and talk, and share amongst us? For me and my brother, we have talked long and often, and there's nothing new in what we say, yet here you are, a real live unicorn, you must be magic, sent to help us too!"

The boy and the unicorn both nodded for the speech was fair and it made sense. And so they talked and it was decided that for now, the unicorn should come with them and live in the empty stable at the bottom of the field behind the aunt's house, and that they would find a way to make things right for everyone.

The sun was low now, and the children knew it was time to return for fear of spending a night not being able to go to sleep for hunger rumbling in their bellies, and so the boy and the girl and the unicorn set off behind the hedgerows to the aunt's house in the village.

But they did not need to fear, for when a labourer came amongst them by incident, he never saw the unicorn;

and when another child crossed their path, hurried and as anxious to be home for supper as they were, the child never saw the unicorn either and they took to the road, and no-one but they could see the unicorn.

And so it was that as the last rays of the dying sun cast long black shadows across a road flooded with orange a cart came towards them, and the cart was drawn by a horse so feeble and so tired that it dragged its feet and would stumble every other step.

And the cart was loaded high, and even higher with heavy barrels and with heavy loads, and a tired workman cursed and flicked his switch without much anger every time the horse faltered and stumbled on its weary way.

And the children stood to one side, and the unicorn stood still in the middle of the road, but the coachman did not see it there, and neither did the tired horse who had been a golden horse a long time ago and now was close to dying of the hard treatment and the work which was far too much and far too hard.

The children gripped each others hands and held their breath as the horse and cart touched the unicorn, then went clear through it, clattering and rumbling dusty on its way into the twilight, fading sound and sight as the unicorn stood, shaken and trembling, in the middle of the road and could not move for terror in its heart.

For, you see, the unicorn had remembered something, had recognised something, but it was too dire and too strange and unicorns don't understand the ways of heartache and of pain, of cruelty and of neglect.

The children went to the unicorn and stood at either side, gently reaching out and touching its neck which was cold with fear and trembling hard.

The little girl asked with much concern, "What is it, dear unicorn? What has frightened you so? We have passed a number of people and a number of carts on our journey so far but here you are, quite trembling all over?"

And the unicorn dropped its pretty silver head and the children could see a tear so shining and beautiful from its great dark eyes, and try as it might, the unicorn could not remain and had to turn and follow the cart that was already a way down the road, and it began to walk slowly and hesitantly at first, then faster into a trot and faster still into a gallop, and then faster still so it was flying across the darkening road and the children ran behind.

The cart had drawn into a lane and up the lane to the ill kept yard of an ill kept house that sat in the shadows of foreboding. The unicorn streaked up the lane, a silver spark in the gloom and the children hesitated at the sharpened fence that bordered what was the dark man's house.

For a moment, they exchanged a glance, but either had to know and find out and be there and neither wanted to lose sight of the unicorn, the first wondrous thing that had appeared to them for all the asking and the praying they had ever done.

So keeping close together and their shoulders drawn in tight, the two children scuttled up the lane like little mice, listening all ears and fearful eyes and pounding hearts for the sounds they might hear and the sights they might see.

The yard was lit by a single tired lantern of yellow light hung from a crooked post. The sound of drinking and men laughing came from the servants quarter, and all alone amidst the cobblestones and the weeds that sprang between them stood the cart, and chained to it still, the worn out horse, its head so low, its back bent deep and no-one there to bring it food or water or release it from its harness.

Beside it danced the unicorn light on nervous feet, big eyes of black ringed white with fear, drawn to what had once had been the golden horse yet not knowing why.

The children crept closer by the stable walls and looked nervously towards the servant quarters, but there was laughing from within and singing too and the door was firmly shut for now.

The children looked at the unicorn and the broken horse and there was something familiar about them both although one was white and light as light would be, and one was merging with the shadows and heavy as heavy could be, yet there was something there that caught the children's eyes and their minds and hearts as well.

It was then that the dark man sitting in his dark rooms felt something that he had not felt in years, and disturbed, he got up and went to the window and looked into the yard below.

And it was then, that the dark man felt a fear he had not felt in years, and he swiftly took his knotted whip and ran down the stairs and out into the yard.

The unicorn and the children startled much at his approach and backed away from him into a corner, backed away from his flashing whip and crunching steps and hoarse voice that filled them with dread as he shouted and threatened them.

"Now I have got you where I want you!" the dark man snarled and laughed as well as he encroached further and further still on the two children and the unicorn all huddled together in a corner and he raised his whip high and with one voice, they called for help to everyone and anyone but there was no-one there to hear them and respond — but was there?

The broken horse had raised its weary head and watched and listened and it saw, and as it saw, deep, deep within itself it found an ember of a long forgotten memory of suffering, and with that long forgotten memory another ember, burning more brightly, of a time before when there was silken grass and wind and glorious racing in the freedom of the hills so blue and green.

And deep within, the ember flared and flared and finally caught fire, caught to life and the horse reared mightily within its harness and with flaying hooves, it struck the dark man from behind who never thought to give the horse another glance so sure was he that there was nothing left within to fight.

Its heavy iron shod feet struck the dark man from behind and he fell senseless to the cobblestones, and as he did, the horse reared up again and screamed such screams as you have never heard, and as it screamed its screams turned into song and this was a song that would fell fortresses and raze the mountains to the ground, and as it sang, the bindings fell from its mouth and shoulders, and as it reared and danced, the iron shoes fell from its feet and sparked lightning against the stony walls, and as it reared and sang and danced, the unicorn leapt forward and it joined the dance and it too began to sing and as it did, their voices blended into one of beauty and of wisdom, and as they danced together, faster and faster still, their forms began to blend and meld and then there was just one horse, golden and beautiful, so much more than either had been, dancing in the yard.

The children stood in awe and looked upon the great golden horse and when the dance was done and all fell silent once again, they ventured forth and both reached out a hand of friendship, and its great eyes, shining with wisdom and understanding and a light they never knew before fell on them with love and true compassion and they knew that it was grateful to them, and that they had been designed to come and start the magic that would set it free from the dark man's spell.

And that was that.

What of the dark man, you might ask? He was broken, vanquished and a shadow of his former self, and when the sun rose high and clear the morning after that, he just dissolved like shadows do, leaving never a trace or a sign he had ever breathed at all.

And what of the horse, and of the children?

They went away together and they lived in the blue mountains, far away.

In time, they would have founded a great city, where you would see statues celebrating the little boy, and the little girl, and the golden horse; and the great city would be known across the land for a place where you would go to stay if you would need to be reminded that there is more to life than toil, and if you look to find your magic.

Sereya's
Song

Once upon a time, in a very far away land indeed, there lived a little girl who didn't speak.

There was nothing much wrong with her, or so we would have thought. She once had a voice and although there was no-one now who would remember how it once had sounded, it might have been quite sweet.

She once had words, too, but now there was no voice, no words, just silence.

No-one noticed this, however. There were many people in the town where she lived. There were mother and father and brother and sister and uncle and aunt and cousin too, and neighbours and people in the church and in the school and in the market square but all these people were talking loudly and living loudly and thinking not at all, and least of all about some little girl that was seen yet never heard.

One day — it was late summer — she stood, as she did, in the shadow of a tree and looked and watched and listened and drank the world all up with her big eyes as she always did. On this day, there was nothing special. As always, people were going about their people business, and the little birds in the tree were going about their bird business, and a dog and a cat in an alley were going about their business, and the tree beneath which the little girl stood was going about its business too of growing and of groaning a little in the wind and of shaking its dusty leaves under the sun. You could say that it was a day like any other but on this day, the little girl came to noticing that no-one knew she was there and that she might have been a rock, or a little tree herself, or perhaps a fence post or a letter box.

This made her sad and she walked away from the town that day, out into the open road and past the fields that were bare and stubbly, with the straw bunched up in rows and scare crows standing all alone, once in a while, and birds sitting on their broomstick shoulders.

She walked for a long time and slowly, it got darker and the sun went down, red and round and then the sky began to show the stars, first the big ones and then the small ones too as all the light went away, as all the colours went away and it was very black and very still.

The little girl was very tired by then and hungry too and her feet hurt from all the walking. She knew she should probably be afraid, all alone out on the dark road with no light to show her the way and the night sounds all around. But she wasn't afraid at all and as it was too dark to see the road now, she went and sat down on the verge amidst some dry grass that smelled nice and was soft under her bare legs and bare arms as she lay down and curled up and thought to go to sleep.

Now, we can't be sure what happened next. Perhaps she slept and dreamed and perhaps the light she saw approaching on the darkened road was real — who knows? But there was the light, far away and to the left, just a shine that lit up the tops of the little trees and the higher bushes that lined the road and it moved this way and that as it followed the winding country road and came closer, closer, towards where the little girl was lying in her nest of late summer grass.

She watched the light come closer and sat up, then stood up to see it more clearly, to see what might be making this golden bright shine in the night that was not at all like any lamp she'd ever seen, much brighter it was and big and round, and finally, up the road came a figure and it was the figure itself that was the light, like the shape of a person but all lit up from within, and the little girl felt a shiver of excitement because she understood that this was an angel, passing by on this road tonight.

The little girl had never seen an angel before but that didn't matter for there is something about angels that is very special and you recognise it right away, even if no-one ever told you that there even were such beings, or if you'd never met one before, or if you didn't even know the word.

When the angel saw the little girl, it stopped in the road and turned to look at her.

It was quite big and it didn't have any wings. It was hard to tell if it had eyes or a nose because it was made all out of light, a light that was alive and bright, swirling and yet it didn't hurt your eyes at all to look at it, which is very different from the light of a fire or a lamp.

The little girl who didn't speak lifted a hand to give a small wave so the angel would know that she had seen it and that she wanted to say hello. She wished she could say something to it and she was afraid that it would think her dumb or stupid and would move along, just like all the people always did, without really having seen her at all.

But the angel did see her, and it raised a shining hand and waved right back at her, and it smiled, too, not in a way like people do but it smiled and she could feel the angel's smile touch her on the shoulder and brush a strand of wayward hair from her face.

Oh, but the little girl wished that she could speak! Oh but how she wished she could tell the angel something, just a little something from all the things that were locked up right inside her mind and in her head, behind her tongue that wouldn't move and her teeth that were like prison bars and held all that and so much more behind it, but it had been such a long time that now she didn't even know how to speak anymore and no words came, no sound was made and she got so afraid that the angel would just drift away from her that she had to cry.

That is when the angel spoke to her but it didn't speak in words or voices but in colours and they made a sense and came straight across to her so she would know its meaning and its purposes, and what the angel said without a word or voice was this:

"Why are you crying, Sereya?"

The little girl Sereya, for that was her name, didn't know what to do because she couldn't speak and didn't know how to make the colours that would tell her story in return and so she cried more, she cried harder, and her hands made strange and pleading gestures to the angel who stood and watched her for a time and then it came forward and picked up the little girl Sereya in its arms of light and lifted her easily off the ground, held her close and without a further word or sound or colour, began to move on, first along the road and then Sereya became aware that they were no longer on the road exactly but gliding above it, and then she could see from the light as it passed below along the road that they were flying, higher and higher still until the land of night lay dark below and there were just the clouds, and high above, the stars bright and white, so many there were, so beautiful they were, and the angel was warm and the little girl Sereya felt entirely safe and entirely enchanted, held close and tight and soft.

For a long time they flew and Sereya might have slept, snuggled close to the warm angel and the music of the stars a rushing that was soothing all around, but then there came a time when they moved in closer to a sense of blue and green, and not long after that, the angel came to set them down on a green hillside somewhere, beneath a blue, blue sky, by the side of a small brook that leaped and bubbled clear sweet water.

Sereya was very thirsty and she drank from the brook, washed her hands and face and all the while, the angel was watching her and once again, she wished so hard that she could speak, that she could ask about this land, where it was, why they were here, ask the angel's name, tell it how wonderful it had been to fly amongst the stars, to thank it for taking notice and taking time — oh! So many things! But still, she couldn't speak and all those things inside of her that wanted to come out, they made a heavy pressure on her heart and although this time, Sereya didn't cry, she sat down on the wonderful green grass and wished she was another, any other, someone who could laugh and dance with the angel, someone who could be worthy of its time, someone who would be interesting, and loved, instead of being good for nothing and with a stone for a heart and the silence.

So she sat and waited for the angel to turn away and fly away but the angel did not turn away, nor did it fly away. Instead, it came and sat down next to the little girl so both of them were sitting in the grass, looking at the little brook as it leaped with joy and bubbled clear bright water.

They sat for a long time, and at first, the little girl was very uncomfortable and got more and more unhappy, thinking that the angel must surely have much better things to do than to be here, and wondering what it might want from her, and how she was doing wrong by not doing anything, and how she didn't know what she could do to please the angel, and all the while hoping, praying, that the angel would stay and not leave her all alone her by this brook, for the truth was that she liked the angel more than anyone she'd ever met and she wanted it to stay, very much indeed.

More time passed and Sereya got so weary with all the worrying that she couldn't worry properly anymore. She found it hard to keep her thoughts as they used to be, here in this beautiful place, where the brook made its little water sounds and sparkled diamond bright in the sunlight, beneath the sky so blue and on the grass so green, and in the grass were little flowers, half hidden, half peeking out with their flower faces, looking at the little girl and the angel who were sitting side by side and watched the brook flow by.

More time passed and the angel hadn't gone away. Sereya glanced at it once in a while but the angel sat beautiful, calm and flowing light right by her side and said nothing in word nor colour, and it didn't even seem as though the angel was waiting for anything, it was just there and seemed to be happy enough to just be there and in no hurry to be going somewhere else.

More time passed. Sereya yawned and stretched out her legs, wriggled her toes and came to think she would like to put her feet into the sparkling brook. She looked to the angel but it was just sitting there so she thought, perhaps it wouldn't mind if she did and so and very slowly and cautiously, she crept closer to the brook, close enough and dipped her toes into the cool and bouncing water.

Oooh! it was cold but really nice and Sereya put her feet right into the brook, until they touched the round cool stones at the bottom and it felt so wonderful that she wanted to laugh and splash, but she wasn't sure if that was alright and she looked to the angel for she was afraid that it would leave if she did the wrong thing but the angel was just sitting and looking at her and the brook and it said nothing and did nothing so she gave a careful little splash with the tip of her toes at first.

The angel didn't seem to mind and Sereya thought that perhaps it was alright then and she splashed very carefully and slowly at first, but it was too much fun and she stood up in the brook, held her skirt up high so it wouldn't get wet and splashed for real, being real careful not to splash any water into the angel's direction because she didn't want it to be angry or upset with her.

But the walking on the smooth stones and the splashing in the brook was too much fun and Sereya forgot for a moment and she jumped up and really — SPLASH! — made a big splash and water went everywhere, including on the angel. She stopped immediately and put her hand to her mouth but the angel just reached up and caught the water droplets in the air with its shiny hands, threw them up even higher and let them rain upon itself like diamonds falling that melted into its warm skin of light and it was laughing!

Sereya watched the angel and very cautiously, very carefully, put her hand in the brook and splashed a little more water across to the angel. The angel bent forward to catch the splashes as before and it was happy and so Sereya was happy too and splashed the angel more, and then the angel got up and put its feet of light into the brook and all the brook became both water and light and they splashed each other, laughing out loud in sound and in colour, and it was wonderful and so much fun, much more fun than Sereya could ever remember having had before.

Exhausted from the splashing and the laughing, Sereya went to the bank of the brook and collapsed into the grass and it was then she noticed that she, too, was now glowing with light across her skin, everywhere where the light water had touched her and that was everywhere, because she and the angel had been splashing really hard and slipped and fallen in the water too between times.

The angel still stood in the brook that was living with its light and it looked to Sereya and then it came across and carefully, touched a light finger to her arm and as it did, something happened and she knew the angels name, and that its name was like the sun but smaller and more joyous too, and it wasn't a word at all but something else entirely and she found that she could think the angel's name and when she did, it made a sound that was the angel's name and it was here, and real, and you could not just hear it but really feel it and you knew completely that it was that one angel's name out of all the many angels, all the across the universe.

And then the angel said Sereya's name, and her name too wasn't a word at all, but it was like a small star of many colours, bright and beautiful it was and it too was what you could feel and know that it was her, just her alone, the name by which she was known entirely and it was the only name like that amongst all the many, many children there had ever been across the time and space of all the universe.

So they said their names to each other many times, and other things besides, and at first Sereya would listen to learn how to say things in this way but as the angel told her many things and showed her many things in its language of light and colour, sound and feelings, Sereya recognised that she already knew this language well, that she spoke it in her dreams and that it was the way that people's words were dead and dull compared to this that had made her give up on human speaking in the first place.

And when she recognised this, and remembered the angel language not just in her mind but all of her, the angel told her that the time had come, and that she was ready once again to come to that very special place of old where truth is told and listened to and where a little girl can tell her story in the language of light.

So they bade goodbye to the brook and the brook sang its delight at having been right there for both of them that day, as they rose and travelled, purposefully and with knowing, hand in hand, across the time and space it takes to go to where there is a place of old, a very special place, high on a rounded hill beneath the stars so bright and watchful there, the sky a colour you have never seen and all the suns of all the time are here, each one a star.

On this hill there is a temple, round it is and bordered by white columns that indeed, are shafts of light that talk to the myriad suns above each one and it was here that the angel and Sereya came and went right to the centre of the temple and this is where the angel sat down at Sereya's feet and where she stood and looked around and then, she told her story in the language of light, and it was a story such as had never been told before in all the times spent, all the days of all the worlds of all the universe, because it was her story and it was unique, as unique as her name in the language of light, which was just like a star of many colours, bright and beautiful.

And the angel listened to her story, and so did the stars above, and the ground below in silence and in reverence and Sereya sang in many colours, many lights, her one voice soaring clearly through the heavens and all the worlds, and it found its place, its rightful place that had lain empty and waiting for her true voice, for her true song, for her true story.

When she was done and all the universe stood first in silent devotion, then vibrated back in reverence and gratitude for all she'd done and when she knew that her voice and being had become recorded in the fabric of time and space exactly as it should, Sereya took a deep breath and knew that she was free and all was right and when the angel took her back to her life in the little town, there was no sadness, no regret and she could speak the words of human language once more, could speak them freely and with ease because she no longer had to try to make it be that language of light she needed to have sung the song of Sereya.

And on a still night, or in a still place, if you just care to listen, you can hear her song, and you can hear the angel's song and all the other songs, each one a miracle and each one so beautiful, it fills your heart with gladness and if you listen even closer still, and if you pay attention, you can tell that one, that very special song of light that is your own.

The
Roach
Master

Not long ago at all, there was a man who had been put into a grim and most horrendous prison for holding views quite contrary to what men in that land were supposed to be holding

Because of his views and because he would not change them, nor stop talking about them, and even other prisoners might be listening and might start to think the wrong things in return, he was kept in a very small cell all by himself, deep, deep in the dungeon cellars, deep below the main prison towering up above.

Here, the sun never shone and there were few sounds; those that were, were far away and deeply distorted.

Here, the man and his views were all alone, and it was a hard time, a very hard time, which grew harder still with each hungry, cold and painful day or night that passed.

It was here that the man began to make friends with the only other living creatures he could find.

Those were the cockroaches that lived in the cellar too; and he would keep a part of his meagre portions of stale slop which wasn't really food at all to feed and train the cockroaches for company and for amusement.

As the years passed by outside in bright spring rains, hot blue gold summers, glorious fire burst autumns and solemn pure white winters, for the man inside, the cockroaches became his world and all there was, and to the others in the prison, even though he never knew or heard of this, he became known as the Roach Master.

But then, so many years beyond the time before which now was all but forgotten, there was a change of rulers in that country and the views the man once held were now no longer deemed to be so dangerous or wicked.

Like many others, the man was to be set free; and a special liberator was despatched to fetch him from his dungeon cell and help with his transition into the worlds of here and now.

At first the man did not know what to do or how to speak beyond a mumbling and a clicking, that was his special language he had used to talk to all his roaches all these years, but with some patience, first the liberator got him used to being in the presence of an other, and then to now remember how to speak and talk and understand.

The liberator then encouraged what had been the Roach Master for so long to leave his cell, to step out to the bright and clear beyond the walls, but here, the man held fast and cried, "How can you ask me such a thing! How can I leave my friends behind, my dearest roaches, every one is named and everyone my deeply cherished child, the brothers of my solitude — I must take them with me, you must find a means of transportation, and if this can't be done, then I'm afraid, I cannot go with you."

The liberator was astonished yet they understood and in return replied, "Dear man, please know and do remember that these roaches are but roaches — they seek to feed, they seek to mate and that is all. Once you are gone, they will continue on their way and do as roaches do, with ne'er a thought of you at all — that love and gratitude you hold them is inside yourself, and nowhere else, and you should never let a love become an obstacle to freedom, and unfoldments of the new."

The Roach Master listened, and thought, and cried a little, but he saw the sense and let the roaches go; no sooner had he opened the small cage he had fashioned and expanded with such care across the lonely, bitter years, than all the roaches scuttled off, one by one, until they were all gone and only little scratchings could be heard; they too did fade most soon enough.

The man who was no longer now the Roach Master, but instead was on his way to find a new name and a new distinction for himself, sighed deeply, shook his head and slowly followed out behind the liberator who was there to steady him against the shock of sunlight, and of bracing wind and clarity.

The liberator took the man in his carriage to the central city, where reparations would be made and bed and food and clothes awaited; but on the journey there, they came across a meadow, beautiful in summer flowers and so green and gold, it made the man's heart glad and he wanted to be there, lie down awhile, and let this beauty aid in his transition and his journey to the life ahead.

They stopped and the liberator was much moved to see the reverence the man displayed and the attention that he gave to grass and weed, to tiny flowers and the earth itself, the way he looked at clouds and skies and to the tree lines, and behind him, blue, blue mountains in the distance far away.

They saw another thing, and it was this which made them smile.

A bird, a dove perhaps, came and it took to land quite close, beside the man, who in response, stretched out an arm in invitation. The dove was acquiescent and it came, short flurry of white wings, and settled on his hand.

The man looked at the dove for just a moment, maybe two, and then he raised his arm and made the dove fly free, and high above.

Darain
Of The
Dragons

It is true that on the day little Darain found the big old strange stone by the river, it was high summer and everyone was hot, tired and bored.

In the summer, when the sun has been sending its rays to the rocks and the earth for weeks on end so you might think that it was trying to melt everything, change everything it touches in its own image, there was little work to be done, for it was too hot to work. There was little studying and everyone was very fed up with the heat and how it made them feel; little Darain's older brothers were no exception.

So when the little boy came skipping through the doorway from the shimmering heat as though it wasn't even there at all, and he showed his older brothers the large and heavy stone he had found and brought all the way from the riverbed that sheltered now only a trickle of water where a wide and mighty waterway would flow in other seasons, they were unkind.

They told him that the big stone was a dragon's egg, they lied to him and told him that he must carry it with him always, keep it warm and sing to it, or else the little dragon inside would never hatch.

The older brothers laughed at little Darain who believed every word they told him, for he was too young for lies, too pure of heart and all things were amazing to him, and magical in every way.

When they told the elders and the others in the village what they had done, the elders did not punish them either; everyone thought it funny that the little boy thus went ahead, carried the big stone with him wherever he went, and sat and sang to it in his clear high voice, and stroked the stone he thought was a dragon's egg, and waited.

Little Darain was a dreamy child, a sweet child, and he took his responsibility very seriously. His little arms hurt, yet he never left the stone behind, and he slept with it too, even though it was hard and cold.

As the days and nights went by in golden haze and burning heat, the people of the village started to call him Darain of the Dragons as a joke and laughed and laughed behind his back, and even to his face; but the little boy simply thought that they were happy, that finding the dragon egg had made them happy, and so he was happy too.

But even the brightest spirit and the purest heart can have their doubts, and as time went by and by, and for a young one, time is near enough eternal and millennia might lie between a single dusk and dawn, Darain began to worry about his dragon egg.

He went to his older brothers and asked them how long it might be before the little dragon would emerge; and once again they laughed and laughed and one said it could be any time, but another said, perhaps it had died inside the egg because Darain had not sang to it enough and it would never now be born.

The little boy was horrified — no, more than horrified for when you're young and pure of heart, the horrors too are near enough eternal and they become the world and everything within, without.

He ran to his room and sat on his bed, with his arms around the stone and sang and sang until his voice could only whisper; and by that time, the night had come and the stone lay as it always did, without a movement, without a single sign that there might be a life within, or ever was.

It was then that the little boy began to lose his heart and faith, and he began to cry so bitterly, because he thought it was his fault, that he had just not loved the egg enough or that his singing was at fault or that it was some thing unknowable, but very bad indeed he'd done and that was why.

"Oh little dragon," he cried although his cries were now a whisper, "I am so sorry. Please don't be dead, I'll sing until the end of days, I promise."

Now it is true that when a one who is so pure of heart is wishing that the wish takes wings, becomes like a bird and takes to the air, the skies, and it is heard; and sometimes, it is heard by someone who is touched by such a plea and on this night, as many falling stars made silver streaks beneath the stars high up above, a being heard, and felt, and it decided and it came.

At first, the little boy Darain did not even see that there was a small light beginning to take shape in the darkened room, for his eyes were so full of tears and his attention on the stone was so complete; but soon enough, the light got brighter, brighter still and then Darain could see a shape of light there right in his room, standing at the foot of his bed, and he was amazed.

As he looked at the bright being, he could feel some of his fear and sadness and heartache begin to dissolve, like ice will thaw when spring has come, and then he heard the magic being speak.

"Child," it said, and its words were like gentle touches, and its voice like the softest music, "I know what happened here and I have come to help you."

Darain was very grateful and relieved to hear the being say this and although his voice would let him only whisper, he replied at once, "Oh thank you, bright light, I have sung and sung and the little dragon won't come out!"

The being looked at the boy for a moment and was much moved by him in every way, then it gathered its power and its magic and it said, "We shall sing together and you'll see, it will. It has been listening to you and it loves your song. You start and I shall join your song."

Darain swallowed hard and licked his dry lips; his voice was all worn out but he did the best he could with what he had and sang the little song he had made, even though it was not much more than a whisper.

The being picked up on the melody and began to sing along, and whilst they sang, it raised a mighty magic and it turned the lifeless stone into a dragon egg, into a real dragon egg, and as they sang, the egg began to rock, and then to split and forth came first a small and beautifully shaped head, with beautiful eyes that found the little boy at once, and they made friends right there and then.

Darain helped the little dragon out of the shell and held it close to his heart, for it was a little wet and sticky, and shivering in the night air. The little dragon was a wonderful colour of shiny silver and it made small noises, which sounded like the song Darain had sung for it or like an echo of his song.

Darain was so happy that he forgot all about the shiny being, and when he finally remembered and looked up, it was gone. "Thank you, bright light," he whispered anyway because he thought that it could hear him, wherever it might live. Then he went to sleep, curled around his own little dragon, and both slept beautifully, and both dreamed with and about each other.

The next day, you should have been there and you should have seen the faces of the brothers, of the elders, of the people in the village!

No one was laughing now, and no one had a word to say for themselves for they were so ashamed for what they'd done. They couldn't understand it, but they did know that something magical had taken place, and that the little boy had made it happen.

The dragon was real in every way; it was small but perfectly formed and very beautiful, and it loved the little boy and would hiss and spit if someone said something bad to him, or about him, or behaved in a bad way when Darain was there.

In time, people became used to Darain and his dragon; and as even more time passed, they became very proud of them both, as many people from far away came to see this wonder.

The dragon grew and flew, and eventually Darain would ride on its back in the skies, free to go wherever he wanted to, free to do whatever he wanted to, with many invitations from the richest lords and ladies, kings and queens in the many kingdoms who all would pay a fortune just to see him and his dragon, just to have him be there and to know that miracles do happen right amongst them, in their own lands, in their time.

The

Magic

Picture

Once, a long time ago, there arrived a traveller in a village which used to stand right here, and he unveiled a magic picture.

It was full of swirling colours, shifting and strangely disconcerting, never standing still and many who came and looked at it thought there was something truly evil about it, a presence or even a group of presences, but even so, they could not take their eyes off it.

They were so mesmerised with the magic picture that they didn't notice the traveller slipping away quietly into the darkness from which he had appeared.

In the fading light of dusk, and then in the flicker of torch fires, the villagers argued.

The priest said he would keep the magic picture in his house to contain the evil.

The Governor said he should look after the magic picture because his house was guarded the most and had the strongest, safest doors.

The teachers said that they should keep it as there may be something that could be learned.

The leader of the hunters and warriors said that it should become a trophy to grace their hall.

The wives said it should be theirs because it was a pretty thing, and such a charming diversion.

The artists said that it would give them much and newfound inspiration.

The clerics argued that they should lock it in their labyrinthine basements and that access should be regulated with permission slips.

They argued all night long and their voices grew louder and angrier as the fires burned lower.

Finally, they fought.

In their struggle, the magic painting broke and shattered into many pieces and each and every one grabbed a part and ran away to take it to their house, and locked the doors so no-one could now take it from them.

The pieces retained the magic and enchantment.

Many years went by, until a group of soldiers, lost upon their path, came across the ruins of the village.

They found overgrown gardens, and long dilapidated structures, silted wells and ruined houses.

But what amazed and scared the soldiers was that in each house, they found a skeleton, or two, or three, and each still held in its bony grip, a dust blind, age flecked mirror shard.

The
Crystal
Magician

Not at all far away from here, there lived a very bad boy.

He did not have any friends, for he wasn't very friendly; and he was always in trouble for the things he said, he did, and others said he did, whether he had done these things or not.

Nobody liked him and everyone found constant fault with him; the people in whose house he lived thought him a burden and told him so in no uncertain terms.

One night, after having done something bad again and having been punished again, the boy had enough and although it was dark and raining, he ran away from home.

He didn't know where he was going and he kept on running and running, through the town, past the farms and further and further still until he could not run any longer and when he finally stopped, he found himself in a dark and dire wilderness.

The boy was very tired and very scared; it was very dark, and cold too, and there were winds and noises all around, no roads, no paths and no lights, just gnarled old trees with tentacles for branches, and hard thorny shrubs that pricked and pulled at his clothes and at his skin.

So the boy could not go on any longer, and shivering he just sat down in the darkness, with his back to an old gnarled tree and tucked between its roots and wrapped his arms about his legs, just to wait for the dawn so he could see again.

That was a hard night, full of fear and many times the boy thought how he had been wrong again, done a bad thing again, and how he would really come to no good in the end, as everyone had always told him he would.

After a long, long time, the sky began to brighten and finally, the day had come. The boy stood up and looked around the wilderness, and it was then that he saw something in the distance, and it looked like a house of some kind. He was so tired and hungry by then that he just headed towards it without giving much thought as to what he might say or do when he got there, and for the whole day he kept on walking through the wilderness without water, food or rest towards the building.

The building was what seemed to be a high tower that showed all straight and square above the waving trees.

As the boy got closer, he saw that it was a large house with a tower built onto it; there were no roads that led to it, yet the tower and the house lay in a pleasant meadow that was not like the surrounding wilderness at all, and it seemed clean and bright, as though someone actually lived there.

The boy snuck closer, very carefully, for he had heard tales of witches and magicians which were said to live in places such as this, but he could see no-one, hear no-one, and when he looked through the windows with the greatest caution and care, he saw a great many good and expensive furnishing and objects, but not a soul was in sight.

He went around the back of the building and when he looked through a window there, he saw into a kitchen, and there was a bowl of fruit on the table, and right next to it lay a loaf of bread on a chopping board!

This was too much for the boy. He tried the back door, found it to be unlocked and ran inside, grabbed some fruit and bread and then scurried under the table to eat it there in big hungry bites and greedy swallows.

He was about to come out to get another piece of fruit and perhaps a drink to wash down this amazing meal when he heard footsteps, and quickly hid himself back under the table, making himself as small as a mouse and as still, with his heart pounding for fear that he would be discovered.

Feet came into view, wearing soft brown boots and a sweeping cloak's hem could be observed from under the table, and a man's gravelly voice who was talking to himself.

"Quick now, quick," he was saying as he walked around the table in the kitchen, "must be away, must be away, to make the most of the light of day!"

The unknown man had collected what he needed and he left the kitchen by the back door without locking it properly behind him, and then he was gone.

For a good long time, the boy remained under the table, far too afraid that the man would come back, but no-one else appeared and the man never came, and so finally the boy came out from under the table, looked around and listened to the stillness of the house.

Now many people had said about the boy that he was way too nosey for his own good, that he just couldn't sit still, always asking questions, always playing with forbidden things, and he stood and knew that it would have been safer to just leave, take some fruit and be on his way, but he could not. He just had to take a look into the other rooms, find out more about this strange dwelling, even though he told himself that someone more sensible would have taken their chance now and just run.

So the boy started to look around the house.

There were many strange and amazing things to be seen, carvings of animals he did not recognise, sculptures of strange looking faces and people, objects that made no sense at all and he had never even seen in all his life, nor even heard about.

There were so many things, indeed there were far too many to pick them all up and wonder what they might be, what they might do, and so the boy just wandered from room to room and here and there until he came to the big spiral staircase that was going to lead up into the tower he had seen over the rooftops when he was still lost in the wilderness.

The boy walked up the first flight where there was a landing and a door.

He opened the door carefully and looked inside — but he could see only empty white shelves and white walls and windows. There was nothing there.

So he closed the door again and went up another flight of stairs until he came to another door. This door was strange and made of thick metal with many rivets; it was held closed from the outside with many fastenings and a big crossbeam.

The boy looked at the door and thought to himself that another boy, more sensible, more intelligent, better behaved than himself would know better than to open such a door and look inside, but as he was not such a boy, he went to the door and set to unfastening all the snapping locks and then he lifted the heavy crossbar aside.

Carefully, he opened the door and looked inside.

It seemed dark inside the room but something glistened and attracted his attention, and so he walked right into the room.

Behind him, the door fell shut.

And in the darkness he saw that the room was filled with shapes, sparkling shapes, frightening shapes but these were not creatures, nor were they demons; these were crystals, huge, big misshapen ugly crystals and they were humming, droning, and as the boy stood and could not move from the spot, they were telling him things, and these were things he had heard before so many times, about badness, and evil, and pain, and suffering and how all things were vile and horrid, and most of all the boy himself.

The droning of the hideous misshapen crystals got louder and louder, filling the boy's ears and ringing in his head, and what had happened the night he had left the house where once he lived occurred again — he somehow jarred back into awareness and he turned and ran to the wall where he thought the door might be, but there were more monster crystals, they were everywhere, their twisted moans and screams clawing at his very soul, but he did not stop and he found the door, opened it and escaped out into the stillness of the stairwell.

For a long time he cowered against the wall, his head hurting, his heart pounding and tears stinging in his eyes, but then he got up and carefully replaced the big cross beam and fixed all the locks to keep all that horror safe inside.

There was the stair well. Another boy would have long gone home, but this one did not. He took a deep breath and said out aloud, "How much worse can it get? I will not leave here before I've seen it all."

So he ascended one more flight of stairs until he came to the next landing. This door was made of glass and it had no lock at all, and when he touched it with an outstretched fingertip, it immediately flew wide open and revealed a most amazing sight.

This room too held crystals, giant crystals but these were incredibly beautiful. Multi-coloured reflections dancing like stars amongst their straight and perfect shapes, fantastic and of such beauty, it took the boy's breath away and he could not help himself, but he had to step into the room, take a closer look, for how could such a thing be real and here?

As soon as he had entered the room, the glass door swung shut behind him and he could hear something — these crystals were singing, softly and harmonic, but yet insistently and their song too was building up and getting louder.

They sang of such things as the boy had never heard — they sang of beauty and of harmony, of colours and of joy, of lightness and of soaring and for the first time in his entire life, the boy did want to listen for these were stories never told, words never spoken, yet these were the things he had always longed to hear, these were the songs he had cried himself to sleep each night for because they were not there and yet a part of him remembered that they should have been.

And as the crystals sang of joy and grace, of splendour and of majesty, of sweeping glory and the pure perfection of all things, the boy found that his own voice joined them in the singing, raw and sore it was at first, but then with gathering clarity as all the years and all the days became undone and made to be a nothing, the boy sang with the crystals and he knew that he had found a gift that was not just for him alone.

How long he stayed there, I don't know, but there came a time when he stopped singing with his voice and instead, his heart was singing.

When that happened, he stood up and thanked the crystals; and without a moment's hesitation, he went back down the stairs and unbolted the door behind which the monster crystals groaned and moaned.

Into the dark he stepped and into the storm of suffering he began to sing the song that he had learned, and as he sang, a wondrous transformation began to occur to the misshapen crystals — they tried and stretched to catch his harmonies in their distorted voices, yet even so, with each one who even tried, the storms of sounds began to drift away as though a wind was changing in direction and with gathering strength and power, all the crystals began to sing the song the boy had brought with him until the song was a movement, then a dance, then a force that melted their forms and gave them a different structure, different existence, which in turn sang clearer and yet clearer still.

One by one, one small shard at a time, the crystals came to life afresh and they began to glow and shine, bring colours and aligning to the perfection and the harmony they found within the song, they turned as beautiful if not more beautiful still than those above them and a unity was born as all the tower rang in song, rang out like God's own bells across the world.

Far away, the magician who owned the tower of the crystals, heard the song and knew it was coming from his home, but he did not know what had happened, and so he hastened back, flying like magicians do across the lands and seas, and he could not believe just what had happened, for he had grown the crystals for a very long time indeed, one set kept in the grim and dark, the other in the bright and love, so that he might compare them and learn something new about the nature of the universe, and how to do much stronger magic.

But such magic as that song!

Already the wilderness had started to transform, already new life began to raise its glory and the oldest, gnarliest trees of all began to sprout new green leaves, and buds that would become their flowers, too.

Entirely astonished, the magician entered his tower, and there he found the boy, and there he learned that only beauty raises beauty, that only truth can call to more, and that the magic he had sought so long was found just nowhere else but there.

So grateful was he to the boy, and so delighted to have found out about his mistakes he was that he at once made a vow to dedicate his remaining years just to the study of beauty and truth, and he took the boy for his son and apprentice, to carry on his work for all the years to follow.

Together, they brought the blessings of beauty and of truth to many; and roads were built, and people came from far and wide to find their healing here and their own voice, and bring the gift of the Crystal Magician to their lands, their loved ones and their homes.

Deep Sea

Jewels

Once upon a time, there was a small village built from grim, cold stone upon a grim, cold and stony shore by a grim, cold ocean.

It was bitter there, bitter cold and bitter hard. The people were desperate and bitter, hard inside themselves and one another, and they never laughed and had no love to give to one another.

Their only source of food were slimly snails and shells they scraped from the rocks; bitter sea weed and most horribly of all, they would go out in their boats and catch mermaids, kill them and chop off their tails for that was like fish and could be cooked and eaten by their starving, hollow eyed wives and pale children.

The fishermen did not want to kill mermaids, but on their stony shores the icy waters were devoid of fish and to survive, that was all they could think to do.

This is how it was; and this is how it had been for all times, for as long as even the eldest amongst them could remember. No-one questioned this life, for they were too worn out and tired by their daily bitter grind and struggle to have any spark left, little wonder as it was.

Every day at dawn, the weary fishermen would put out their ill-built boats out into the stormy ocean, to begin their awful task of catching mermaids for their tails again, just as it was and how it had been for all times remembered.

But one day, one time, there was a single one amongst them who found a young mermaid in his net and she was crying, near to death, and when he raised his knife to cut her from her body, his hand was stayed and he simply could not do it.

Knowing that releasing her would bring even more suffering and hardship to him, his wife and his starving children, he untangled her from the net and placed her back into the water, and he said, "Swim far away, to live or die, for I can no longer kill the likes of you to sustain my own miserable existence. For sure, I'd rather be dead by a well aimed, clean cutting butcher's knife than suffer on — this trade is not worth it."

The mermaid heard him and felt his terrible sadness and his desperation, but she did not understand such things; deeply troubled by it, she swam to the deep reaches where the elders resided and told them what had happened, what she had heard and what she had felt.

The elders sang together for a long time, and finally they all rose up and swam out towards the bay where the fishermen's desolate village lay, and when the fishermen put out the next morning in the freezing mist to once again find sustenance and survival for another weary day, they were met by the merpeople.

The merpeople told them that they knew of a place where treasure lay and offered to show them the way, but the fishermen were afraid and suspicious.

They had killed so many of the merpeople that they thought the merpeople must be their bitter enemies and that they had come to lure the fishermen into a deep and vicious vortex that would suck them all under for revenge.

So they refused to go.

But the one whose hand was stayed had nothing left to lose, and he alone followed them in his small boat.

Out to sea, far out to sea they went, further than the fisherman had ever been before, and further still, but he never lost heart nor hope, for he had none to lose. He simply followed and at last, at the far horizon, there was an island.

As he came closer, he could see that all the white beach of the island was covered with the most beautiful jewels, deep sea jewels they were, washing up with every tide from the mountains deep, deep below the waters where they had slept since time began.

In the white sands they lay and sparkled — precious diamonds, sea green emeralds and flashing high sky sapphires, royal rubies and the deepest, richest golden topaz, of colours true and pure that sang and touched your very soul.

The fisherman whose hand was stayed fell to his knees in the tide and raised a handful of them to his eyes, and then he cried, and then he was confused for he did not know that feeling which befell him — not having ever known a single moment of happiness before, how could he have known?

Eventually, he turned around to thank the merpeople, but they had gone; he took a fraction of the never-ending deep sea jewels back to his village, and it changed everything for everyone.

Not only were these jewels precious beyond imagination, but their very purity and beauty made a healing for all who beheld them, a soothing of worn brows and tired backs, a wind of light to stroke a bent head and a vibrant dance for bringing aching feet to life.

For the first time in their terrible existence, the people of the village were happy and joyful, and being joyful, there was no longer need to hit and hurt each other, to take from each other, or to grate against each other like the boulders in the sea will turn to sand.

The villagers took their jewels then to other places; and in time, a great fleet of pure white ships with the whitest, billowing sails would sail the oceans near and far, bringing jewels to the farthest reaches and taking goods and payments in return.

And on each ship, high upon the highest mast, a silk flag was flying, embroidered in the finest, richest colours — bearing an image of a mermaid, and a fisherman.

In
Sanctuary

Once upon a time, in a far away and very peculiar kingdom, there lived a girl.

Now, she was not your usual child for she was head-strong and not at all as nice girls should be; and she demanded far more of the world around her than was seemly.

She constantly complained about the lack of love, the lack of care, the lack of attention; she asked for things, and when she didn't get them, got furiously angry and screamed most loudly; and worse still, she often refused to do things she considered to be stupid, boring, painful or pointless.

She was a very difficult girl.

In the peculiar kingdom in which this girl lived, it was held to be best practice to make sure that all children grow up and expect nothing, want nothing, hope for nothing and desire nothing at all, lest they would be disappointed, and the adults there were adamant that children had to learn this early on, so that they would grow up and never question that there was no point to anything at all, at least not any kind of point that would make any sense to anyone with half a brain.

But try as they might, and they did really try with all their might to make the young girl behave herself, she just wouldn't stop complaining about the things she didn't want to eat, to hear, to understand, to see and to feel.

So she found herself, young as she was, at war with the entire peculiar kingdom.

This war started first thing in the morning and as soon as she got up, and it really never ended for as long as she was awake, and even though her life really was a nightmare, she just couldn't stop asking for a different world, a better world.

When she got old enough to carefully creep down the bottom of the stairs and sneak out of the back door without anyone observing her and catching her, so that she might be put to some new work or lesson that would teach her how to behave correctly in the ways of the peculiar kingdom, she went outside and there, she found a better world, just like she had always been insisting should exist.

Outside, and far away from all those peculiar rules and regulations, tasks and demands, there was a different life.

There was a sky with clouds that could be anything; and these clouds never screamed at the little girl.

There were trees and grass and flowers, and these would never ask her to start digging, chopping, cutting, working.

There was a little brook with quick and lively water, beautiful in sun or rain, and it just flowed and giggled and it never once looked at the little girl full of resentment or reproach.

There was rain which fell from the sky and never complained how dirty she was, or how ugly; it tickled and slid cold in pretty drops over her skin and nestled in her hair and it didn't care at all to tell her to be quiet when she felt like she wanted to say something, or to sing.

This new world which lay both outside as well as within the borders of the peculiar kingdom was everywhere, and there, the little girl found a place of freedom, joy and wonder, and she would do just what she could to make it so that she could go there as much as possible, for this other world had healing powers, and if she could be there just a time within each day, then it was easier to stand against the torrent of abuse and rage, neglect and sheer insanity that was the order of the day, prescribed by law for all the citizens within the most peculiar kingdom.

The new world gave her strength, and that was not at all what those who tried to train her in their most peculiar ways would like to see, for they saw it as being all their tasks to break her from her strange ideas and have her be the same as all the other children who sat pale and quiet, lied and learned to lie until they knew no longer truth from fabrication.

So it was decided for her own good — so they said — to put her in a place where she could not escape; where there was nothing but the walls and many other children being trained all day and most the night to be good citizens of the peculiar kingdom.

They put her into a prison cell and locked the door.

The girl, she cried; she raged and shouted, but it was to no avail. The walls were solid and the doors were solid too; there was no window and the world outside was now no longer there to help her, give her strength and the reminder that there are quite different ways of being, doing, feeling and experiencing this life.

She cried and screamed for many, many days to no avail, and then a dark night came upon her and she might have been re-educated at that moment, but when it came, and when the question came as if she only had imagined all that other life of joy, of beauty and of freedom, and that it really wasn't there at all as all the other, bigger ones had always held and always sworn, it was as though a light streamed right into her prison cell and she…

REMEMBERED.

She remembered the feel of wind in her hair, and the heat of the golden sunshine straight into her back and radiating hot and golden through and through, into her arms, into her feet; she remembered the little brook and the sweet clear water, flowing always, endlessly, uncatchable, and then the rain, the diamond little spheres and droplets, making perfect circles in a puddle; she remembered the earth soft giving, slippery between her toes and she remembered the colours when the sun goes down, more radiant, more beautiful than all and anything the lost ones from the kingdom had to offer or did think so valuable, or so precious.

She took the memories and lovingly, assembled them in time and space within her mind, within her being, and she held them there and clear and bright, and there it was, her world, her one and only world, and it was there, and it was with her even here in this dark night, in this dark prison cell of stone.

The world of beauty, it had come to her; and once this happens to a little girl or to a little boy, it cannot be undone, not by a thousand beatings or a million insults; it cannot be undone by pain, by suffering, or by the many, many words, no matter if they are screamed right into your face or softly spoken sneaky poison dripping guilt and shame.

The world of beauty, which the girl decided to be known just as the real world, it had come and never did it leave the little girl again. Eventually, her strength was making all the teachers and the trainers weary for they did not have such a power, such a magic and such truth to nourish them or to sustain them, and their fear would go so far, but could not ever stand against the power and the beauty of the sun and rain, of trees and little creatures, soaring birds and mountain rock, and deep inside they knew this too.

They had to let her go.

The girl went back to her old home in the peculiar kingdom and went on with her life.

It was hard, and it was difficult, and she never did stop complaining about the miserableness of it all that everyone seemed to take for granted still, but she had found herself, had found her world, had found her freedom and so everything was really, quite alright.

Hero of
A Thousand
Wars

Just the other day, in a place not far from here, there was a city which had decided to celebrate their heroes, special soldiers who were called in when there was a disaster or an accident.

These special soldiers were very brave. They would go where others would run away, into burning buildings and very dangerous places, to assist their fellow citizens.

Not long ago in this particular kingdom, there had been a big disaster where a huge palace had been destroyed and many had died and perished.

Quite a number of the special soldiers had come from this one city in which our tale occurs; here, the city managers invited them all to this big party and to stay at their most glamorous inn, give them lots of food and speeches for the gratitude and admiration of the people in the city were great.

Preparations went underway. Garlands were hung in the streets, "Welcome Home Hero!" signs put up all along the main road, the children and the adults all were given a day off and flags to wave and flowers to strew into the hero's path.

So there was the grand parade, and all the heroes arrived at the inn — but then disaster struck again.

There was no water in the inn at all and not a place for the heroes to wash up from their long journeys and the long days. Being heroes, they didn't grumble or complain, but all the organisers were rushing around most upset with their heads burning like torches for the embarrassment of it all, and because they felt they'd let their heroes down.

Specialists were brought in but they shook their heads sadly and proclaimed that it would take at least a day to fix this so that water would be available in the inn again.

One young counsellor had an idea. He suggested that people from the city should adopt a hero and invite him to their homes, let them use their bathrooms, give them a welcome and assist them right now. Then the heroes could go on to the party, which could be moved to another building soon enough, and things would be well after all.

This was announced to people of the city and to the heroes, and a big cheer went up from both parties. Two lines were formed, one for heroes and one for citizens with bathrooms; pairs of people would meet up, shake hands and then the citizen would take the hero back to their home.

One lady citizen was immensely excited to get to take a hero home. She was most admiring of their work and courage and stood in her queue so impatiently that she nearly seemed to be dancing. But when it came to it, and amongst all the excitement and upheaval of the day, the man she was to take home didn't look like a hero at all.

He was very dirty, he smelled bad and although he wasn't old, he didn't look quite right at all. In fact, he so didn't look like a hero that in a heartbeat the young woman understood that he might well be just a homeless man, of which there were many in the city, who had taken this chance, this opportunity, to get himself invited into somebody's home.

For one moment, the young woman didn't know what to do. But then something strange happened, and she never quite knew what it was, never managed to work this out, not even much later, but she stepped forward, held out her hand, shook the hand of the dirty man and spoke the words of "Welcome, hero." She led the way to her apartment which was right next to the centre of events, and the dirty man followed.

She spoke kindly and showed him to her bathroom. She also gave him some clothes that would fit him, as he was very thin and quite small, gave him her best towels and her finest soaps and then sat down outside the bathroom to wait for him.

The dirty man had never said a word. Whilst the water was heard to splash and rush, the young woman sat outside and wondered about herself, about this man, but she still felt very strange and so she just sat there.

Eventually, the door opened and the man stepped outside.

He wasn't dirty anymore. His long hair was combed and wet still from the water; his skin was clear, his eyes calm and beautiful and when he smiled at her, she knew that he was indeed, a hero of a thousand wars and that she was blessed to have been able to assist him on this day.

The young woman stood in awe and didn't know what to do, but the man went towards her, smiled at her and said in a calm and beautiful voice, "Thank you, Jenny."

Then he walked past her and let himself out of the apartment.

For a moment longer, the young woman stood in shock and then, something broke and she rushed to the door.

"Wait!" she called out, "Wait!"

But when she looked down the corridor, it lay empty, and silent — there was no-one there, no-one there at all.

The
Fairy Gift

Across the oceans wide but still upon this very world, there lived a woman with her family.

The lands she lived in were pleasant enough; in the spring, all was green and pleasant; in the summer, golden and hot with deep blue skies above; in the autumn, there were splendid colours in the trees and soft sunlight sparkling between the leaves; and in the winter, snow would fall and turn the world to white in crystal beauty.

There was no war, her family was all alive and everyone had time to play as well as work and one might think that this woman was grateful, happy and lived a very good life but I'm afraid that wasn't so.

She would moan and whine, complain about gravity and how hard it was to put one foot in front of the other. She would complain about not being respected enough, not loved enough; and basically it could be said that nothing ever really pleased her as it should, no matter how pretty, bright or sweetly sensuous it might have been.

Now don't get me wrong, this woman was not at all a bad person, or wanted to be miserable all the time. It was just that she always felt that something was missing from her life and although she tried to be happy as best as she knew how, true happiness eluded her, no matter what she tried to have it be that way.

One night, the moon was full and round and very, very white, she looked out of her window and sighed because she wanted to go out for a walk, hear the trees whispering softly in the night air, and feel the breeze against her cheek, the misty moisture soothing her skin, her hair; but she felt too tired and too despondent to make the effort. She would have to get up, find her coat, find sturdy shoes and she was already worn out from a day that once again had been far too long to keep on trying to pretend that she was happy and content.

She looked through the window pane at the moon outside and she became very sad, much sadder than she normally was, and this time, she didn't have the energy to fight that old familiar sadness and she started to cry, big round tears that flowed like rivers, but why she cried, she did not know.

Now there were tears as well as the window pane between her and the moon outside and that was just too much to bear. The woman finally got up, put on her coat and her sturdy shoes and quietly, as not to disturb her husband and her children and the family dog, she slipped out the door and into the night.

As soon as she had taken the first steps away from the house, a great relief and a feeling of peace came to her and she knew she had done the right thing. She began to walk down the street and towards a place where trees were growing still and where one might forget for just a moment that all around there was just so much stone and metal, people stacked on top of one another, in their millions, mostly sleeping now.

Soon she arrived where the trees were still; and she went and stood amongst them, with her hands in her pockets, looking up at the moon and wondering why she had come, and what she could hope to find.

But here was a magic; and here I tell you that the woman on this night had heard a call to bring her here. She hadn't heard the call with ears, you understand; it was a magic kind of call that one hears with the heart and then your heart must lead the way and you must go and all the thinking you might do won't do a thing in any way.

And so it was that in the grove of trees a light began to shine, and on this night before the eyes of the astonished woman something did reveal itself and shimmered into being — a finer, higher light that did not blind her eyes but that was soothing and entirely fascinating.

The light grew denser and it formed the shape of what appeared to be a small girl, or perhaps a very tiny lady and the woman drew a breath in shock because she knew and recognised from somewhere old and very old this was a fairy — and it had come to meet her and to talk to her!

The woman stood stock still but shivered with excitement. She did not dare to blink her eyes for fear that then the fairy might just disappear and it was all a dream — but then she heard a singing, a fine sweet voice and she did not understand the words with her ears, but with her heart and her heart grew strong and joyous for it had been waiting for a song like this forever and a day and never had it given up the waiting or the hoping that the day would come.

The woman was immensely grateful just to be there and she wanted nothing more; but the fairy had a gift for her that went beyond the gift of being there — and what a gift that was already!

The fairy produced a small cup without a handle or a stem; perfectly shaped and rounded at the base, and it seemed to be made of living light, and from inside it, tiny shiny things emerged and sparkled up like the bubbles in champagne and it was magic manifest.

The fairy held it out to the astonished woman and sang a something that would let the woman know this was her gift and she should take it, make it all her own — it's yours, I've come to give you this, accept this with my love and joy.

The woman was completely overcome by all of this but her hands moved all by themselves and opened, held out in a gesture of acceptance, and the fairy smiled a radiance and placed the magic cup into the woman's hands.

The woman took it, took it close and held it to her chest. She tried to formulate a way to thank the fairy but the fairy was already singing a farewell and with a shimmer, it was gone.

The night lay silent, save for a hush in the stately trees, and the woman's breath that left a plume of white.

She looked down and there was the fairy cup in her hands. It was quite real, felt cool and lively all at once and there were those fascinating little lights that sparked from deep within — and she knew that this was fairy dust!

The woman touched the fairy dust with greatest care and an outstretched fingertip.

Her finger sparkled for a moment, there was a sweet and lively small sensation that travelled right up her arm and into her very core and it was gone.

And then the woman laughed aloud and the sound of her laughter rippled the trees and the night, and the moon heard it too and was delighted just the same.

She took the cup and carefully placed it in the pocket of her coat, held tight by her hand wrapped around and tingling from the fairy dust, and as she walked more lightly, swiftly, than she'd ever walked before back home she had a thousand ideas of where to brighten up her world and bring a sparkle of life and joy and lightness to her home and those she loved with all her heart.

The
12th Spirit

Once upon a time and in a land that was not unlike ours in many ways, it came to pass that one of the ruling groups had fallen into disrepute; and all the members of the group as well as their families were being hunted, jailed and killed for all manner of evil doing they may or may not have committed.

As luck would have it, one young man had been away on travels when this had happened; and when he came back, he found himself a sought traitor, with a big price on his head and his family dead, his lands in ruins.

In great fear of his life, he fled.

There was no safe place left for him to go to; there was no-one who would offer him shelter, take him in or hide him, and so he went north east, as far as he could go, into an old, old forest, where no-one lived at all and no-one had lived for as long as anyone could now remember.

He walked and stumbled for many, many days; his only food was berries he would find, and other fruits of the forest; nuts from the abundant trees, and water, fresh from the small rivers there.

He wasn't used to hardship, and although he was a sensible young man, he had not used his sensibility for much other than for leisure and for pleasure in his life.

Here, in this vast, old forest, where the first leaves were falling gold and red and made his footsteps hushing, rushing reminders of his flight, he was at a loss more profound and more lonely than he had ever known.

But he kept on walking as there was nothing else left for him to do; and when it rained, he would sit beneath a bush or in the shelter of the roots of a great tree and huddle in his cloak, that once had been the height of fashion and was never meant to be his only blanket, only means of dryness, warmth or comfort in the world.

The nights were cold now, and the mornings were of mist and chill; still, the young man walked on, lost in the forest which took away the thoughts and feelings about all those things which were now of the past and all those things that once had been, and now no longer were for him.

How long he walked, we cannot know; but one day, and as the morning had long given way to gentle sunshine streaming through the oldest of the trees, he came upon a clearing, where grass grew luscious and the green of luscious bushes reflected in the surface of a deep, still lake.

By the side of the lake, there were the ruins of what must have been a large and stately building once; now, there were walls still standing, and stones thrown here and there; between them there grew forest flowers and a host of berry plants, all greater and finer looking than he had seen elsewhere in the forest, and as though this was a place of magic, where magic flowed from the very ground below and gave all living things a special charge and sanctuary where they may flourish to their greatest height and realised potential.

When the young man saw this place, he knew at once that it was most enchanted, and he knew at once that here, he had found a home within the forest, that this place would help him rest, and heal, and that it would now take him in and give him shelter, that his long journey of confusion had finally come to an end.

For the first days, and how many there were we cannot know, he simply slept and rested in the ruins. He found a part where something like a house did still exist, and three of four walls were still standing.

There was a hearth, still stout and bearing an ancient chimney, and a roof above; he collected dry leaves to make his bed and be his blanket too in the coldness of the nights, and then he set about to look around, to see what he might find and that might help him live here and survive the coming winter.

He found old pots made of earth and clay to carry water in; he found pieces of wood to burn in the hearth and even found a rusty old sword which he laid aside with a notion to sharpen and clean it with a stone in the coming nights of winter.

All through this time, he slept deeply, never dreamed and in the days he didn't think of anything at all. In the silence of the forest he simply lived and worked to make this place a home as best as one who has no knowledge of the ways of home craft, carpentry or masonry might manage.

He collected berries and roots and nuts to dry and store, and one day, as he explored the ruins, he found beneath a layer of creeping vines and dark green ivy what appeared to be a set of steps that led down into the ground, in darkness.

He was excited by this discovery; there may be hope of stores of things, and some might still be now of use to him, and so he fetched a little burning wood to be his torch and climbed the stairs of stone with care as they were covered in debris that had been falling there for many, many years.

The deeper he went, the less the leaves, the little sticks and stones became and then, there was only dry dust remaining. He found a pathway, deep below, with a rounded ceiling made from big and finely fashioned blocks of stone, and he followed through this passage way until it opened up into a chamber.

This chamber was empty, square in shape, save for a single old and very heavy looking set of shelves made from sturdy old black wood at one end.

He was not disappointed or disheartened; this place was very old and it would have been most surprising to find anything at all, so he counted his blessings to have found the heavy wooden shelves and thought that he could use those to make a front for his apartments, to keep out the wind and snows which would be soon to come.

So he put down his piece of burning wood and tried to move the shelf, and move it he did, and when he moved it, he saw that there was a door hidden behind the heavy shelf, and that this door was made of metal, not of wood, and that it had a great locking bar which secured it from the outside.

"What might this be?" he wondered aloud to himself, and set about trying to raise the crossbar which was most ancient and quite rusted into the iron hinges which were holding it in place.

But finally, the crossbar gave way, and he pulled the door open.

There was a strange movement of air, very cold air that made him shiver and feel most disconcerted for a moment, but then he got his piece of burning wood and stepped inside the room he had discovered.

And there, on the floor in a large and wide room, deep underground, there lay the skeletons of monks, still in their cloaks, a great many of them, with their heads close together and their feet pointing outward, and their bony hands still folded on their chests as they had been for an eternity.

The young man stepped back and stared; he breathed the cold and dusty air and felt the stone floor spin beneath him, and to centre himself and regain his senses, he counted the bodies of the monks.

There were eleven, all told.

He looked around the room and saw that it was orderly and tidy in all ways; and he saw too that there were candles still, unlit and dusty; that there were books that even still below the dust showed shining glimmers of their gold leaf bindings, and there were treasures, paintings, altar pieces made from precious metals too, stacked neatly in the corner of the room.

Slowly and carefully, he walked around the skeletons in their brown robes, and as he did, it struck him that they were quite small and slender; these had not been adults, but youngsters, acolytes, and not grown men as first he had imagined.

The young man did not know quite what to do.

He had no wish to be intruding here, or to disturb that which had happened here and which seemed to be still happening within this room; and knowing not of any purpose, he decided to leave all just as it was for now, and so he closed the door again and even placed the heavy shelf back in its old position, climbed from the cellar and sat by the lake in the late autumn sunshine, thinking not at all and simply watching the reflections on the water, deep gold and golden red.

There, he fell asleep on the soft grass, and there, he dreamed a dream.

And in the dream, the centuries rushed by at speed, and once again, the past was here and now and long ago was real, and what was now a ruin was a monastery, built to worship God in deep serenity, and there were roads within this forest, and further out, castles and villages, full of life and full of people doing what they would and always had.

There was a school here where the ones who felt the calling would assemble and the older ones would teach the younger, songs and stories, prayers and what wisdom they had found themselves or heard from others too.

There was a war, and soldiers came; and as the young man dreamed he saw all things now unfolding, as the older monks hurried the young ones to the cellar hiding place with all the riches they had to protect; and there, they shut them in and told them just to pray and not to fear, so they would all be safe and that no harm should come to them.

But the soldiers came and they slew all the monks, and everyone around they butchered too. They searched the monastery, took what could be taken, but they never found the acolytes nor all the great and wondrous treasures that were rumoured to be hidden there and in anger, they set a fire of revenge upon the monastery so that it was destroyed.

All who knew about the hiding place were dead; and it was locked not from the inside, but from the outside, and so it was that no-one came to finally release the boys who sat and prayed and waited there within.

Days passed and then, their food and water was all gone; but still, they talked amongst themselves and they gave each other solace, and they prayed and sang together, and when one amongst them cried in fear or hunger, all the others would combine and tell him of the love of God, and that all things would be well; and so they did not lose heart, nor did they lose their hope, and even after long they knew that not a soul would come now to release their bodies so that they may live a life within this world, they did not fear, nor did they cry; they prayed and sang and talked of God and all the glories that awaited them, a different kind of freedom.

As they got weaker, and then weaker still, they lay down together on the ground, close and with their heads together so they could whisper still and hear each others voices in the dark, and then they went to sleep and they began to dream together, and in their dream, they died together, but never knew that and so still, they lay and dreamed of God, and all the glories that awaited them, a different kind of freedom.

And their dream was so beautiful, so restful and so healing, so relieving of the burdens of fear and nights of darkness, loss of hope that when the young man joined their dream, he too began to understand a great many things about his life and that of others in a different way, and he too began to raise and rise within himself, and when he did awake, he was a different being by his meeting and his dreaming in this most enchanted place.

All through the winter, when it came, he slept and dreamed the dream together with the others, and as the snow settled thickly outside, he would do his work of keeping clean and alive, warm and safe, and then lay down to sleep and dream again, and it was there that he brought his existence then into the dreaming circle, all the things that he had known, and felt, and tasted, touched, experienced; and it was there that then the others understood that they were dreaming still and had not realised that they were dreaming, for he alone did wake, and wake again, and eat, and fuel the fire, mend his clothes, and shine the rusty sword with a soft stone most lovingly, and gather wood, and melt the snow for drinking and to wash his body.

All through the winter, the dream expanded and it deepened; and when the young man walked on virgin snow, mystical mornings of blue and enchanted hues of rosy red beneath the distant sun, he would not walk alone, but all would walk, and all would feel, as all would dream when he lay down and closed his eyes, when night had come and stars of radiant light would bless the sky above.

And then, the snow began to melt; the sun grew stronger and the first and finest blades of grass reached green through crystals left of ice; and then the young man knew that time was right, and time had come; and when the ground was soft again and flowers bloomed amidst the glade and ruins, he lovingly and with the deepest reverence, and with his own hands, dug the soft dark earth and made eleven graves, all side by side.

And he went inside and with the greatest care, enfolded each of the small bodies in their cloaks, and carried them outside, and laid them there into the ground, and covered them most gently over, so that they might rest and that the dream would now become reality.

Each one he knew, and each one he knew by name; and when the last one had departed, the young man too stood up and blessed this place with all his heart, and left on his own path, to be a king.

The Book
Of Law

Once, there was a planet, and on the planet, there was a single city.

In this single city there lived very honest and hard-working people, and these people had most special and specific codes and rules of regulations as to how things should be accomplished; what to think and how to act in any given circumstance.

These people had religion and they had their gods; of course, they had so many rules and regulations that would guide their path and way there too so that not one amongst them ever could get lost, or even have one single moment of confusion.

Amongst the many things these people did in their most careful and most patient way was that they kept extensive records of the times gone by; and all and everything they did or any of them did was always well recorded, catalogued and archived in the most exquisite manner, so that not ever even one thought, or a single thing would be misplaced or lost.

All these and many other things they did according to the rule of the Book Of Law.

Outside the city walls, there was the graveyard.

The first who ever lived within the city as it was and had been now for many, many thousand years lay buried with their headstones closest to the city walls; and those who had once been their children lay a little further out, and so it went, along and further through the generations upon generations, each and every one accounted for, and each and every one laid out exactly as the book of law decreed it should be done.

And so the times went by and on and on did stars and comets whirl within the skies, as season followed season followed season, on and on, and on they lived and on they died, until the graveyard had encompassed all the land they had and it took many weeks now for the journey out beyond the city and then back again to bury all their dead, as it was done according to the Book Of Law.

Of course, they could not stop their living or their dying; so they built ships and as the centuries, millennia passed and passed again, and further and still further came the road and greater and still greater spanned their graveyard across mountains, deserts, forests, steppes, savannahs, even swamps and over hill and vale, and still they kept on going and recording, just as they kept living and then dying, as they always had.

And then the day it came, when all the planet was now an enormous graveyard, and there was not one single plot left anywhere at all to place a body, not a one; not on a mountain slope nor even in the darkest underground, for they had filled it all.

This was a dire moment and the elders of the city held a council in their crisis; and as they no longer had the option of the burial of the dead as it was stated in the Book Of Law, they felt that there was only one way out of this — that they would have to be immortal.

If they did not die, then there was now no need for further room or further graves; and as their science and their magic was now old and strong, it was decreed.

Upon a day, all people in the city gathered and a mighty spell was made; and each and every one of them became immortal, stuck in time as they now were from then until forever, and that was how it came to pass.

They never added to their number, and it was not until a hundred thousand years had passed again that others came in ships of fire and of steel to visit this most awful place, where all and everything was nothing but a grave-yard, and where insane and twisted creatures roamed between the never ending rows of crumbling headstones, and amidst the dusty remnants of the archives in the city of the Book Of Law.

News of the existence of the nightmare place that was the home of the immortal city dwellers spread amongst those races that traversed the stars.

There was much fascination with the place and many more amongst the beings who lived far and wide on many levels, many planes came forward and they said that they had visited this dreadful, dusty place of death in dreams and visions and had always wondered where it might be found, and whether it was them who were insane to be experiencing such things, and feeling what they felt when they had touched the dire suffering that radiated far and wide across the times and spaces of the worlds.

And so it was that now more visitors arrived, in many different kinds of craft, in many different ways that different peoples had for travelling amidst the spaces and the planes; and many visitors had many different reasons that would make them undertake the journey.

One race of beings made a point of adding such a visit to the educational curriculum of all their youngsters so that they might learn the difference between unfoldment, and stupidity; the elders of that race were most delighted to have found such an impressive and persuasive case in point.

Large groups of youngsters would arrive most every day, and shielded in all ways would then observe and be succinctly terrified as well as greatly educated by their visits.

But there were others, not quite so good and friendly in their motivations; there were tribes amongst the planes who came from most impoverished environments, came from places where there was simply not a lot to eat, or mine or trade; and these would hear of graves that spanned entire continents and all they saw or thought was treasure, jewellery and precious objects and adornments they could dig up from the ground, blow off the dust and sell to others who collected prizes of this kind.

One such tribe made straight for the forsaken place upon receipt of news of its existence; their craft was very old and very much constructed from many rusty and ill-fitting pieces, held together just by clever hands and clever minds that could take anything at all and make it work for them.

They were a ragged bunch of many different peoples; they had sought and found each other and for many years had worked together and established trust to a degree, and some were young, and others old, but in a way, they were a family that stuck together for survival.

Their ship arrived and entered in the atmosphere; they cautiously flew low to find a place to land and could not really then believe their eyes and their receptors when it was all quite true and real — there wasn't anywhere at all that was not covered in these graves, row upon row, line upon line, each headstone just the same as every other now, all covered in the dust of ages, all exactly the same distance from the next, and not one inscription was still legible for they had long since worn away to nothing.

They landed their craft amidst the fields of the dead and exited with caution and some overwhelm.

Where should they start?

It didn't seem to matter much so they began to dig, and it was so that where they dug, and absolutely everywhere they dug, they found what they'd been looking for — a clasp of precious metal, or a ring; a staff, bejewelled; an ancient and exquisite knife; there were tiny sculptures made from luminous crystals and from beautifully coloured stones, and hardly any bones remaining still or strands of hair or any of those things that normally made robbing of the graves into a less than pleasurable experience.

To be fair, the ragged family could not believe their turn in fortune.

This was too easy, and most wonderfully easily rewarded, and what treasures did they find!

Just one day's worth of digging and they had assembled more than any of them ever hoped to find in an entire lifetime rushing here and there, and facing danger, hardship all the while.

And so, and quite in spite of all the myriads of graves surrounding them, regardless of the dust of death that lay and swirled and was disturbed and then disturbed again by all their digging and their running, they were more than merry, and they laughed and yelled across to one another, held up high the latest treasure they had found, and their bright voices of so many different races, accents, tones did ring across the endless valley and it was, that they were heard.

Far away, on the slopes of a mountain where head-stones were slipping now and precariously shifting, tee-tering, one of the ancient city dwellers raised its strange, disfigured head with eyes that saw not graves or dust, but mostly past and sometimes an abyss of everything, or nothing; and it felt vibrations and it wound and twisted for a while at this unknowable intrusion, and as it wound and twisted it came closer to the source of the distur-bance, drawn most irresistibly towards events that were, when nothing ever was, or ever could have been...

The dusty and exhausted but most jubilant group of reclaimers had heard the eerie noises and howls in the distance, and of course, they had noticed how throughout their day of digging and of finding treas-ure upon treasure, these howlings were growing closer, and more closely still.

From all around these sounds did seem to echo, and to the band of reclaimers it did sound as though there were many beings, many angry spirits gathering to take their lives, to take their souls, to take revenge for the transgression they had most certainly committed here.

And yet the sounds they heard and thought to be the sounds of many, not of a single one who was approach-ing whirling, rotating, flailing round and round, in spirals widening now and then decreasing yet again, did neither frighten them too much nor did they stop from digging and reclaiming; they were a fierce group and they had suffered much already, they were hardened, and they also were most deeply now determined to take advantage of this extraordinary offer to take the present, and from what their actions were, to shape a future that was different, and brighter.

They had weapons, and they had courage; they trusted one another for they were more than brothers now, and they kept alert and most aware whilst digging, sorting, carrying swiftly, and adding to their treasures and their riches with each moment, movement that would bring them more, and more.

As night began to creep in, steadily and stealthy, gently and at first, unnoticeably obliterating outlines in the distance, softening, encroaching all around until the widest sweeps of the eternal graveyard could no longer be discerned, and more, until the reach of awareness had receded so that only around the portable sources of light they had set so they could see the graves, and each and one at all, so too the many howling sounds drew closer, nearer and it seemed that they were always just beyond the border where what you might see did merge into what you might not; and finally, the leader called a halt and said they needed rest, and to get themselves prepared for what was surely now to come, the sounds now being very close indeed, so close that even the most stalwart of reclaimers shuddered, peered into the gloom and dark and lost their concentration on the many treasures that were waiting still within the dusty ground.

They gathered closely around their illumination and they argued — should they leave? It certainly would seem the safest option, and it was most certainly the truth that they had gathered treasures of such kind and such variety that each and every one of them would live like kings from this day forward.

Yet some did argue that they wished to stay.

Some argued for their greed; some argued for the fact that even greater treasure might be shared with others on the worlds they left behind and would alleviate a lot of suffering there; some argued for they did not like to run away, and thought themselves more honourable if they would stay and face the unknown spirits, alien entities or enemies of dark which were well near upon them now.

And as they argued and their voices rose in anger and in volume, it was then that from the dark, there burst the citizen into their circle made by light.

It flailed; it twisted; it moaned and screeched; it was a sight of such extraordinary wrongness that the reclaimers stumbled back in terror, and they clung to one another even as they drew their weapons, raised them high and aimed them at the being but they saw that it was simply flailing in an agony that wasn't of their making; that it was writhing with its twisted limbs in no direction, so it seemed, and that it wasn't seeking them to hurt them or to drive them out, for it was totally insane and such purposes were now no longer even a reality.

They saw its cries and moans, they saw its twisted pain, they heard and understood a fate that was of suffering and of endless dissolution, and hardened as they were, the suffering of this tormented creature touched their hearts and one of them then fired at the creature, and not from anger or from fear, but from nothing but a pain of wanting there to be an end.

The fire from his weapon struck the creature in the side and it screeched and burned, and screeched and reached and twisted, but it did not die, for it could not; the magic it had made so long ago still held its spell, still held its power, just as it had, for all those unknown times.

The others, horrified beyond what they had thought could put a terror in their hearts, now also fired at the being to give it peace and resolution; and although their weapons burned and tore, the creature would not, could not die although the damage now was thus that it could cry no more, nor could it move.

The reclaimers were speechless, thoughtless, entirely overwhelmed with this event that they in truth could never understand, and yet they saw, and felt the creature's suffering as though it was their own, and they stopped shooting and approached it, stood in a circle around it, brought their light and stared at it and then each other, and they did not know what to do.

Until a one amongst them, for what reasons we can never know, began to sing a song in a most unsteady voice, a simple song that he remembered from his world, from times ago, a song that they would sing to children in the night so that they would become most still, and unafraid, and close their eyes, and sleep in comfort.

Some of the others knew this song as well and as they could not think what else to do, they too joined in with their rough voices, unused to singing and a chorus formed and rose above the body of the being that could never die.

But what they did not know was that this song they thought to be a simple children's song was magic, was an ancient incantation, written long, long ago by beings wiser, older than they ever now remembered, and what they did not know was that this song contained the antidote to the very magic that had created all the suffering in the citizens, and what they did not know was that the ancient ones had made this song on purpose just the way it was, just for this moment, for a time like this exactly, a most fantastic gift of healing passed amongst the generations, carried all across the stars with each and every person who remembered it, held it inside themselves and thus, could pass it on — exactly as had happened here.

And so, and as the group of vagabonds did stand around the creature in the circle of their light and sang the song, the ancient spell was broken; and they saw that from the broken, twisted shape another did arise, a misty white, a shape of a being pleasant, well constructed, beautiful, although they did not recognise it as any race they'd ever seen, they did admire it; and limited as though they were in their experience, intellect and comprehension knew nonetheless that this was what the creature once had been, and now could go on to become again, in a different way and in a new way all at once.

The spirit of the citizen did rise and waver, and when finally it became aware and knowing of just what had happened here, it gave a blessing and the gratitude that fell about the reclaimers was an endless ovation of love the like they'd never known, and then the spirit of the citizen rose up, high up into the night, to find the others of his kind and bring this blessing to them all as well.

The twisted creature was dead.

The reclaimers stood in silence, for there were no words to tell just what had happened here. When finally they broke their silence, they said very, very little, but instead set out at once to make a grave for the being's broken body.

They used their machines to make it deep, and wide; and one by one, they brought all the treasure they had taken back from their ship and placed it in this grave, every single last piece of jewel, ornament and treasure, and there wasn't one of them who held back or kept a single item, not a single one.

They worked through the night and when the day came and brought its light, they were finished; there was no headstone to mark this grave but they gave care and heed to smooth the dusty ground and eliminate their tracks and all the evidence they ever walked upon this ground.

And they returned to their ship when the sun was high, and they went away.

They never spoke of the treasures they had left behind, but it was strangely so that from that time, this crew of reclaimers found themselves recipients of much good fortune in a multitude of different ways.

Those who had secretly hungered to find love did find it; more than they had ever dreamed or hoped of. Those who had longed for fame did find it easy, as did those who wanted wealth; it was as though what they had taken had been given for their service in that night had made a change that was unlike the change you find in treasure.

And what of the world itself, the world where once there stood a city, the city of the Book Of Law?

Strangely, it became quite forgotten by all and every-one who'd ever heard of it.

Strangely, if you were to take a chart of stars and look as where to find this world, there would be no name and no direction; and even if you asked the ones who really once had visited there about this world, they would gain a distance in their look and shake their head, and then they would forget the question too and go along their daily path.

Star Child

There once was a time, and there once was a place; and this place, it was a great meadow by the side of an old forest of the darkest green with the tallest trees which lay around the flanks of great soaring mountains like a royal cloak.

In this meadow, there lived a woman in a house that was golden and warm; bright and airy, snug and cosy and just decorated enough with loving touches to make this house into a home.

The meadow was beautiful, as was the valley beyond; so were the great forest and the mountains. The air was bright and clear, just as bright and clear as the fresh brook which ran through the meadow, bringing the finest, most delicious water from the springs high up above; and always, the skies were radiant, in dusk or dawn, in rain or snow, in highest summer sun and just the same when diamond stars were whirling up ahead.

And yet, and even though she lived within this blessed land, the woman was unhappy, for she was lonely and she wished for nothing more than to have company, to have a child to care for and to call her own, that she might have a reason in the mornings to arise and someone to whom she could sing songs and tell the ancient children's tales.

Night after night, and day after day, she would cry and weep and pray for a child to come to her, for a miracle to happen; and after many years of crying and of praying, it was by chance that a most radiant being passed that way and heard her distant cries.

The radiant being came swooping closer, in long, drawn out spirals, closing in and down until at last, it did emerge upon the meadow, just behind the house where once again, the woman lay and cried and prayed.

The radiant being made itself known, and the woman was most astonished but also most delighted, for everyone who cries and prays deep in their heart of hearts do hope that such a thing will happen, that a radiant one will come; for else, what would the purpose be?

The woman started to tell the radiant one in a great flood of words and of gestures, of expressions about her plea but of course, there was no need for that at all, and the radiant being made a slow motion which silenced the woman instantly, and then it spoke to her, right deep into her mind and it told her that it was on a far mission, to find those who would take care of a star child for a time, whilst the star child was still small and needed just such care; but that there were certain conditions that would have to be observed.

The woman was overjoyed and cried out immediately, "Oh yes! Oh yes! I'll do whatever it takes, whatever you want; I will be a perfect mother to the star child! Whatever the conditions, I say yes!"

The radiant being understood that the woman's need was great after all those years of crying and of praying, and it was very kind but firm and it told her that the conditions were important, and that no star child could be given to a home without it being absolutely understood what was to happen, and agreed upon by everyone in every way.

The woman nodded and even though she was full of dancing impatience, she understood that the radiant one thought this to be important and that no star child would be had unless she listened, and she did, but only just with half an ear as the radiant one explained the child would be with her only for a certain time and that she must be prepared to give up the star child when this should be called upon to do.

"Of course! Of course! I'll do everything I can to be the best, the very best mother any star child ever had!" the woman cried and then she held her breath for fear the radiant one might change its mind, but it did not.

The radiant being told her to prepare a room, a bed and told the woman that when the day after the next would come to show the first of the night stars close to the horizon, it would return and bring the star child for her care taking.

"Oh thank you! Thank you!" the woman cried but even before the first "thank you" had faded, the radiant being had swept upwards, outwards and away and was no longer to be seen.

The woman scrubbed and cooked and cleaned and prepared and she was so full of excitement that she could not sleep at all; and the afternoon of the second day seemed to take a dozen lifetimes as the sun crept slowly across the sky and finally, it disappeared in gold red glow behind the mountains and the night came, velvet and purple, and there was the first star twinkling bright.

As the woman watched the star, she saw that it grew brighter and then brighter still, and there was the radiant being, swooping in and down, and in their arms, it carried a small child of such beauty and such glory as you have never seen.

The woman wept like never had she wept when the radiant being placed the child into her waiting arms; but this was not the usual noisy crying that the woman had been practising for all these years, instead these were river tears of joy and gratitude and admiration as she beheld the star child in her arms.

It was perfect, alive and radiant with light, and this was a light that touched the woman's heart in the most strangest of all ways, and it touched her soul, and touched her mind, and all her body, all her being like a song — and then there were no longer any tears, just joy and gratitude in radiant glory as the woman looked up to see the radiant being there and she thanked it with all her everything for having being given this the greatest gift of all.

The radiant being was still and beautiful, and it reminded the woman that she should take good care of herself and of the star child, and also that she had promised to give it up when the time had come and the care taking was complete, and the woman nodded and assented, and the radiant being left, up and away into the starry night.

And so the woman and the star child lived in the house in the meadow, and it was a wondrous time, a perfect time for both, and the star child grew from a tiny infant to a young child, and it was full of joy, always, and every thing the star child did discover about the world in which they lived, the woman too re-learned afresh and often so it was that she herself was yet a child again, a one who never saw the snow so white and perfect, crystalline, alive; a one who never felt the touch of rain upon their face, or wind trapped in their unbound hair, or smelled the forest, dark, and green, and old.

The star child was happy and it thrived most beautifully. It made friends with creatures in the meadow and in the forest, and wherever it went, it seemed as though the very rocks and roots and earth below took on a finer, softer, and more perfect radiance.

The woman too was happy beyond measure, and she too did thrive most beautifully; and so time passed, and then more time; it slipped down the stream from the mountain side; it melted like the clear, tipped icicles in spring; it rushed like autumn leaves and crackled like cosy fires in the hearth when storms came sweeping down across the meadow.

And one summer's night it was that the woman and the star child were sitting outside in the meadow together on a blanket and they were watching falling stars when one grew closer, brighter, and it was the radiant being, and it had returned to take the star child home, for so the time had come and time was here, and now.

You and I who tell and listen to this story, we cannot know just how the woman felt when first she saw and recognised the radiant being; just what the woman thought or how her heart seemed close to bursting when the radiant being spoke; but even so, it cannot be a great surprise to learn that here and then, the woman told the radiant being that she could not honour that which once she promised and that she could not let the star child go.

The radiant being stood in silence as the woman told of her decision; it showed no sadness, showed no anger nor compassion; it just told her to consider that the star child's journey was still young and only just begun; and that it was time now for the star child to go forward, home to where the star children go and grow when they become young star people, where they meet their own kind and take forms and shapes that never would we guess or know about.

But none of this could move the woman; she could not bear to let the star child go and so the radiant being left and for the first time since the first night she had held the star child in her arms, the woman cried, deep bitter tears of pain and fear, and fear of loss, and so the star child did become most greatly troubled and alarmed, for it loved the woman well and most in all the world and wanted nothing more than that she should be happy, as they always had been up until this night.

The woman and the star child talked all through the night and to the dawning of the day, and the star child told the woman that it did not care for stars, or anything beyond the meadow and the forest, and the mountains, and that it would most gladly stay right here for all the times from here into eternity, if only that the woman should be glad again and never more, no longer sad.

So they remained, but things were not as they had been before.

Soon after, it began to rain, much harder than it had ever rained before upon the meadow and it simply would not stop. It rained and rained and rained and after many days and nights, one night, the radiant being came back and it spoke to the woman and said, "It is raining because the world is crying. There is no star child in the heavens to watch over it, and the rain is its sorrow."

But the woman shook her head and said, "The world does not know what sorrow is, nor how many tears I would cry if the star child was taken away from me. I will not give it up."

The radiant being went away, and it continued to rain and rain, and no flowers blossomed in the meadow even though it was now spring, and no birds were singing anywhere.

After many days and nights, the radiant being returned again and it spoke and said, "The birds are no longer singing because their voices reach into the heavens, and there is no star child there to listen."

But the woman shook her head and said, "The birds may be silent, but they don't know just how I would cry to the heavens if the star child was taken from me. I will not give it up."

The radiant being went away, and the rain continued, and there were no flowers, no birds, and finally, after many days and nights, the sun did not rise any longer in the mornings, and all was black for all the hours.

After a time now no longer counted in days and nights, for there were none, the radiant being returned to the house in the black meadow and it said, "The sun will not rise any longer, for there is no reason for it to rise and shine, as there is no star child in the heavens to see its light."

But the woman shook her head and said, "The sun may not rise, but it doesn't know what happens to a heart when it is broken and all the light has gone, as mine would be if the star child was taken from me. I will not give it up."

The radiant being went away, and in the black meadow the rain continued, and all life slowly sank into cold, and into darkness, and extinguished one by one; and with every life that left, the star child became paler and less bright, and less joyous, and at first, the woman didn't notice this but then she did, and when she did, she opened the door of the cottage to the black cold everlasting night outside, stepped out into the everlasting rain and called to the heavens, called for the radiant being, and said that she was ready at last.

The radiant being came, and the woman fell to her knees and said, "I can live with forever rain, and I can live with forever night, and I can live with nothing alive but I cannot live if that means that the star child should suffer, grow paler and disappear. I understand now the meaning of love, and of care taking. I am ready for you to take the star child."

The star child ran to the woman and it assured her that it didn't mind dying for her, because it loved her so very much and would do anything to make her happy; but this time the woman shook her head and said to the star child that she would be happy only if she could know that all was well for the star child; that it should grow up to become what it must and always should have been; and that she was so deeply sorry that it had taken her so long to understand that.

So the star child went to the radiant being and they stood next to each other; and it was so clear that they were both one and the same and of the same kind; and the woman bowed her head to them both.

The door opened; outside lay the black forever night and the radiant being took the star child by the hand,

and they turned and walked out into the darkness. The woman scrambled to her feet and ran after them; she was just in time to see both be like lights and swoop up and away, far away into the black night; and where their light went, the clouds parted and the stars were shining brightly, and it was there their pathway and their travel took the lights they were until you could no longer be sure which star they might have been.

The woman stood and looked up into the night sky where the clouds were ever more receding; where the rain had finally stopped; and she waited for her heart to break and for her end to come; but instead, she felt as though her heart was expanding, getting bigger and bigger, wider and higher, reaching up and out and far away and when it was as big as all the worlds and all the suns and all the stars, it was then that she found the star child again, and she understood that it was never meant to be taken from her, and that it was now always with her, and not just this one star child she had been so privileged to take care of in her own life and with her own hands, but all the star children, all across the Universe.

The Heart Of The Desert

Once upon a time, in a very far away place, there was a great golden desert.

It was the most mysterious place on the planet; for no-one who journeyed there too deeply ever would return. It was vast, and sweeping like an ocean, from one end of the horizon to the other; it was very hot in the day and bitterly cold at night, and very few creatures or people lived even in the outer reaches.

What lay in the centre of the great golden desert, no-one knew at all.

Yet there were stories.

Stories about cities that lay beneath the sand, and graves of kings of old; of mysterious wells that would restore health and youth if only one could drink from them, and gardens, the most amazing and splendid gardens with fruit the likes you have never tasted, and flowers the likes you have never seen, where one might live in joy and gladness, and forever.

These stories were told, and over the many years, the centuries and millennia, travellers and explorers would come, fortune seekers, adventurers and sometimes men and women who had nothing left to lose, and they would go to the small towns at the edge of the great golden desert, and they would trade what they had for beasts of burden, water, food; and they would set out to seek the treasures of the desert.

Some returned later, dry and dusty, desperate; some were found by caravans, half dead and raving; and most were never seen again.

And yet the travellers came, and still the merchants would sell them gourds and skins with water with a sigh, and make a sign of magic and protection, for themselves and to allay their guilt.

On this fine morning, glorious and bright, with the sky so blue and the sands in the oasis white and sparkling like snow, the tents and colours bright and fabrics blowing in the breeze, three new travellers arrived.

There was a young man, and a young woman and an old man with hair of white; they looked like a family and rode on fine horses.

As they made their way to where the merchants sold the things one had to buy before one tried to enter and to find the heart of the great golden desert, many eyes were watching them; they may well have been a king and his son and daughter, and many sighed and shook their heads, and all thought that like all the others, they were doomed.

But what they did not know was that the old man was no king, but instead, a mighty and powerful wizard; and the young man and the young woman were his best apprentices, smart and strong, and that the wizard had been waiting for many, many years to find the right ones so that he could make his age old dream come true and find his way to the heart of the great golden desert.

For many years, he had studied and studied; learned all that one can learn from fairy tales, from songs, from stories, drawings and letters sent by people long ago and from the dusty archives of the past.

For many years and many nights, he had studied maps and studied them again; so many maps, drawn by so many hands across the ages, but all were guesswork at the best; and much fantasy as all the map makers filled the most mysterious and quite unknown white spaces in the centre of the desert with their hopes and dreams, and their imaginings and sometimes, with the demons of their fears of the unknown.

For many years and many days, he had waited for an apprentice to come to him, just the right one, who would balance and support him on the quest to finally reach the heart of the great golden desert and to see for himself what the truth may be; many apprentices came and went and finally, he understood that he had made a mistake in waiting for just a single one; he found two, who together had the skills, the powers and the resources he had sought for so long.

When this day had come, he was finally ready.

An old man now, but not old enough to be incapacitated, just at the right time all these things, they came together and so it was that on this bright desert morning the magician from a far away land where there was mist and rain, and ancient forests deep and green, and castles built from strong stone and iron grey rode into the border town, flanked by his young apprentices, and in their packs they carried not supplies but magical items, for it was the old magicians supposition that it wasn't water that would take them to the heart of the great golden desert in the end, but something altogether different.

Still, they did stop at a merchant's tent and there dismounted to acquire just a sensible amount of fodder for the horses, to refill their stores of way bread and for one last rest and civilised refreshment here before their journey would begin in earnest; and the old merchant who had seen so many travellers come and go, and never then return at all sighed, as he always did, and most especially about the young man and the young woman; full of life and very beautiful they were, childish in their ways and much like brother and his sister would behave with little jokes and tricks they played upon each other all the while.

He grew so fond of these two that he warned the old magician one more time; he asked him seriously and in a low voice to consider all the folly of this undertaking, and that he should not and never put his children thus at risk.

The old magician laughed, for he did understand that the merchant must have made the error of assuming that he was the father of the two, and told the merchant not to fear, that he had studied this a long time and that he was sure as sure could be of their success, and that indeed they would return and promised as a jest to tell the merchant first of all and in all preference just what they'd found, and what they'd seen, and bring a trophy for a gift, especially for him.

The merchant did not share the old magician's humour and light heart; he shook his head, and sighed, and prayed to his prophet to protect him from the hurt of all these people who would never listen, and would all excitedly, go straight out there, into the fierce and never ending desert, and there just find their end, in pain, starvation, dehydration and the madness that the burning sun brought to these fools who would delude themselves that they could be immortal.

And as he watched from the shade of his tent as the three re-mounted and began to make their way due south, into the desert, he kept on praying but his prayer changed for one of mercy, and protection for them all.

So the magician led the way and his apprentices followed; and they rode into the desert, due south, the only direction which could take them straight through the heart, the centre.

Very soon, the outpost town behind them dropped away to nothing; and the endless desert stretched out before them.

Very soon, the heat became unbearable and the three stopped and from their saddle bags, produced special magical cloaks with hoods they had carefully fashioned before they left on their journey; these where a silky white that shimmered many different hues beneath the sun and not only did these keep them cool and protected inside, they also helped the horses and so the three made good progress.

Here, at the start of the journey, there was a trail still visible.

Many feet and many hooves had left impressions in the sand, and soon enough, they passed others, other travellers who had set out on days before them, grimly struggling along, their eyes scrunched up against the glare but looking to the south without a fail.

No words were exchanged, and the three never stopped; and when night fell, they made their first camp and rested.

The stars came out, bright and brilliant, and it became cold; but the three magicians did not notice beneath their magical cloaks and instead, they brought forth maps of the heavens and compared the stars above to these; and discussed amongst them how to best proceed from here.

There had been a plan, quite vague but this was now beginning to take shape more strongly in the old magician's mind. He did not tell his apprentices as yet; they needed to travel a little further before this plan could be engaged.

But it was decided to now travel in the night, not in the day; and when the day came then to rest beneath a tent made of the magic cloaks, and shelter their fine horses there as well, for that would be more comfortable and sensible by far.

They set out again long before dawn and made good speed; and once again, they passed more travellers, more weary still than those of yesterday, and when the sun became too harsh, they stopped and made their camp and rested well until the evening came, then night and travel was once more a pleasure under deep black skies, a brightwhite moon and the sands beneath them like a purple ocean.

So they travelled for three days, and then another three; and on the last of these days they saw no-one any longer and the path ahead lay clear and wide.

It was on a night that started rich with shooting stars that the old magician placed his staff into the sands and said, "Tonight, and here, I will evoke the spirit of the desert."

The two apprentices looked up with interest and some astonishment, for he had never mentioned this before; but he did not explain to them. Instead, he looked up at the sky and walked away from where they had made their tent to spend the day, away from the trail and out into the desert, following a star that sat high up above the low horizon, twinkling bright and beautiful.

The two said nothing and they simply followed too and so they walked an hour, maybe two, beneath the holy silence in this strange and inhospitable land, leaving trailing footsteps in the sand to mark their passage.

Finally, the magician stopped.

He looked around and spoke a spell, hushed into the silence and a light shone from the end of his staff. With this light, he inscribed a large circle, and then three further circles inside that, all touching; and he beckoned his apprentices to stand in one of the smaller circles each, before taking his place in the last remaining one.

He turned to the girl and said, "Sing the song of the desert."

The girl was a spell singer; she had a great talent for listening to creatures, to the land and all there was and from what she learned to make a song; her voice was pure and clear and ranging wide in tones of fine distinction, and when she heard her master thus instruct her, she smiled and closed her eyes and was most glad she had been given the permission to do that which she had wanted to be doing since first she saw the desert stretching far and wide — to call its name and sing its song.

She closed her eyes and let her senses range far and wide, up and down and in and out, and draw right back from every day so that there was no longer any thought remaining, any barriers or noises, voices that could stand between her and the ancient desert, and finely first, then gathering in strength there came a stream of information to her, through her and her voice responded and she did begin to sing, fine notes and sounds that made a tapestry, and rang and found a harmony with all around them and with her companions too.

The magician and the young man too now closed their eyes and entered into the singing stream, and their voices too joined in and added their existence, made now their presence known to sky and star, to all the ancient land and ancient sand, and above all, now the magician's call began to rise as he invoked the spirit of the desert, ancient guardian from times past, times here and now, times still to come; and all three gave their offering of love and admiration to this world, which was a world within the world yet different from the many other worlds that they traversed, a world with laws and with potential, a world with destiny and with design that they had come to know and learn, and on this night, to worship.

Their song was true, and it was real; and so it was that the spirit of the desert heard them, and was touched and was awakened, and it was drawn to that which sang and asked for interaction, for union, for attention, and it rose up and gathered from the desert, rose up from every single grain of sand and even from the ancient waters, way below; from the ancient rocks far deeper still and rose and gathered to a form that did become more dense and more aware as it came closer, swooping vortex and the centre was the circle of the three who knew and felt the spirit's rising and responded with delight, with joy and with excitement as they felt the spirit's power and desire for this meeting, for this union of such different souls, such different beings, here united on this night so that all may share, and learn, and change perhaps; a ritual as old as life itself and just as holy.

The spirit came and swirled around the three, swirled through them and it sang as well, it joined the song, a voice so rich and so unique, so powerful and wonderful that nearly did they falter; yet all three were full of trust and of desire and they held themselves within the spirit's wind; they held their song and sang within their limitations of their youth and simply being human and that was enough to make the tapestry of union then unfold as all ceased to remember who or when or what, and all was song, and song was all there was.

Another desert morning, fine and bright again saw once again the border town come into life and long before the sun had risen.

The old merchant opened up the sides of his tent so that what breeze there was may pass most freely and he made to dust his wares when he saw from a distance shapes and shadows were approaching, coming from the desert, from within.

He froze and stared and tried with his old eyes to see the best he could, and tried to work out what he saw; horses, were there two, or three?

Was it the old man and his children, now returned in safety and come to sense and sensibility?

Did they turn back and end their folly, so that they could live a life, and the old man would live to see his grandchildren play and call his name?

But as the movements grew closer and clearer in his vision, he could see that there were four horses, not three; and that only one carried a rider.

He ran his hands over his tired eyes and shook his head, and wondered why he would have such affection for these people that he had only met the once, and how it was that he would think and think again about them, and now feel such heartache, deep inside.

Eventually, the single rider, dusty, tired and exhausted, burned in face and hands and all that still protruded from the silken cloak the man was wearing, made his way to the merchant's tent.

He fell upon a trough of water, with the horses right beside him, and when he had regained his clarity and his composure, told the merchant he had found three horses sheltering beneath a tent, close to the trail; that there was no-one to be seen and only footsteps leading off, into the desert.

He told that he had followed the footsteps for an hour, maybe two, to offer his assistance to a fellow traveller, but they had simply ended; one moment, they were there, the next, there was nothing at all, just the sand.

He spoke of calling out and waiting, wondering, and then returning, following his own and the departing footsteps back to where the precious horses waited patiently and it was then, he said, that he had understood that he could not continue on this journey, on this quest; that he would take these horses back so they may live, and take himself as well, so he may do some living of his own.

The merchant listened with a tight heart and with all intent; he feared this man might be a robber who had slain the old man and his children, but as he listened, and as he learned, he grew to believe what the dusty traveller was telling him, and he agreed to trade for the horses, and the many mysterious objects which included the cloaks and immensely valuable ancient maps and parchments.

He gave the traveller a good price, not exactly fair, but as he was a merchant, that was all the way it should be done, and the traveller left with gladness and completely new ideas of what his life might be, or what it was about.

And as he tended to the fine and priceless horses, the merchant fell to musing, and he wondered what had happened, what became of the old man and of his laughing children, and somehow, somewhere, he had this feeling that the old man had just kept his word, and sent a message as he said he would, and that indeed, the desert had a heart, and that it can be found, was found, by those to whom the calling was much more than just adventure.

The
Wedding

A time ago, and it may have been long or no time at all, there was a day one day, and on this day, there was a wedding.

People were running here there and everywhere with flowers and with great green swathes cut from shrub, bush and tree; with garlands and with table cloths; with food to be cooked and food to be prepared and food already made; setting up tents, and chairs and tables in a sweeping garden on the green, green grass in brilliant sunshine, and the sky was blue above, without a cloud; radiant blue like the most precious of sapphires.

The sun was sending down its golden rays and warmth to all and everyone who was so hard at work to make this wedding extra special and a feast to be remembered right into old age, and possibly beyond.

On this bright early summer's day, it was still morning, and the bride was in her rooms.

She was a princess born; so young, and so very beautiful, even though she only wore her underwear for now, and all her hair was tied and screwed up with many holders and rags, piled on top of her head, and she was rushing here and there, her face aglow just like a lamp, and her sisters and her friends, her mother and her aunts were rushing all around as well — oh! It was chaos!

Women's voices everywhere, a squealing like you'd hear from all the way across the valley, and everyone was tripping, falling over one another and their clothes and items as they tried to get themselves and the young bride to be most perfectly turned out and perfectly on time for this her great event and for the coming celebration.

Across the valley, in a big stone palace, there was a similar scene but here, the ones who did the stumbling and the rushing and the swearing were all men — here was the bridegroom, young and beautiful he was, even though for now, he only wore a shirt and socks, and a towel on his head, and all his brothers, cousins and his friends, his father and his father's father, and all his uncles too and though they tried to keep themselves all steady and most practical, they too were falling over one another, trying to find this or that and oh! — It was chaos!

Fluttering excitement lay across the entire valley, and absolutely everyone was milling, rushing, for this wedding was a special one, a one that would unite two great and ancient houses who had been at war with one another for so many years that many thought they'd been at war with one another since the world began, and everyone was invited.

Everyone was invited to the wedding.

Of course, all the lords and ladies had long received their beautifully drawn and painted parchment invitations, brought by well dressed and important messengers into the many fine and multi-splendoured drawing rooms, in castles, palaces and country houses.

Of course, all the merchants and the guild professionals, the doctors, teachers, scientists had found their envelopes with printed invites on the entrance tables of their stout and steady houses too.

The clergymen and women, shoemakers, blacksmiths, bakers, tailors all had been invited too as had been all the guards, policemen and the soldiers and their officers from the opposing sides but still, it didn't stop with those.

The farmers too had been invited, and not just rich and prosperous farmers and their families but all the farming folk, and even the indentured workers on the land were told to come, and all the other workers, servants, stable boys and girls and those who herded sheep and goats; and even the lowest of them all, the tramps and vagrants, the children from the orphanages and the paupers from the poorhouses were all invited to attend.

And to make sure that no-one, and most absolutely no-one was left out, it was arranged to have some special cake and food delivered to the prisons and the hospitals so that the ones that really could not move from where they were could also celebrate the wedding and partake in the entire valley's joy of the event and the occasion.

And yet, and far away and on the furthest reaches of the valley, where the mountains grew stern and most forbidding, rising grey clad high right up into the clouds and topped with brilliant ice that never melted, there was a one who had not been invited to the wedding.

He lived all by himself in an ancient tower made of old stone, so old that it was black with age and no-one knew who built this now; it was a dark place, and an ugly place, so no-one visited it ever and indeed, the valley folk did not come near it so they wouldn't have to see it even, and to shudder.

This man was once, the brother of the king whose son was to be wed this day; but long ago he had been cast away from family, and home and hearth; the doors were closed to him and servants were instructed not to open them, nor even recognise his name, his face should he approach; and he was driven out in deep disgrace.

He was most bitter, twisted, lonely, full of raging hatred at this treatment though his actions had been such that it might well have been deserved; and all those many years spent brooding and in isolation had done nothing to improve his temper or his disposition.

Most times, he kept himself as deeply and as absolutely focused as a man can be on studying old books on magic and by reaching up and out, beyond, below, to find a source of power for himself that he could use to shape his life, as all the other powers he had once possessed or hoped to gain had been removed from him and made impossible to be attained.

He thus was a magician; and much power he had now assembled in his endless, sleepless days and nights inside the tower black and cold.

Each morning he would go up on the highest turrets of the tower and he would look down on the valley, green and golden, beneath the sky of purest blue and on this day, he saw that something was most different.

There was movement everywhere; it seemed as though the valley was in motion.

This perplexed him and he brought forth a powerful telescope so he could look and see what was occurring; it had been many years that he had used it for it was most painful to the man to view the valley people go about their business and to know that he could never enter there.

He placed the old telescope on the turret, cleaned the lenses and began to view and see the movements, all those people, all those carriages, like ants so far away they were and yet all were streaming towards the central plane, and when he trained his telescope upon that place, he began to understand and know just what was happening, and that here was an event for all the people in the valley, and that everyone had been invited to partake — everyone, of course, except of him.

And on this early summer's day, it then became too much for the magician — all of his hatred and rejection, anger and his envy at the people living bright and pleasant lives out there broke loose from deep inside him, where they had been chained like demons in the vaults that lay within his heart, and they came roaring up and to the fore, and on the spot, he swore that he would take their festival, and that he would tear it all apart, and make them weep and wail, and teach them some of what he knew of suffering, and of despair.

He called up all his magic and his power, like never he had done before, and he opened up the gateways to a place he had discovered on his journeys, a place he thought was hell, and he stepped into this place and there, he gathered all his forces of conquest and doom, to strike just when the moment was in absolute perfection.

At midday precisely, when the young and brilliant early summer sun stood high and radiant above, and all the many different peoples of the valley had assembled at their best and finest, on a beautiful, round marble platform that was supported by many sweeping columns and which had been constructed so that everyone could see the wedding, even from a long, long way away, the prince and the princess stepped up together to be wed.

Side by side and perfect each in youth and beauty, decked with the riches and the symbols of their state and of the day, they walked along a priceless carpet made of red gold and strewn with many flowers, straight towards the very centre of the platform whilst choirs of children in white were singing and the kings and queens and courtiers looked at them in rapture, and in admiration.

They walked towards a plinth behind which the most important of the clerics of all the valley waited, dressed in golden robes and shining in the sun, to speak the words and make the vows that would bind them both, and through them both, bring peace and progress to the valley the likes of which had not been known before.

The young couple was most serious and as beautiful as anyone could be; the prince could not help glance at every stride most swiftly at the princess who was as a goddess on this day and not a girl at all, or so it seemed to him; and to the others who were watching, it was more, much more than just a wedding.

The royal pair arrived before the plinth; they halted; the choir fell silent and everybody held their breath as the cleric raised his hands in the ancient gesture of blessing which from the days of old would set the wedding ritual in motion, when…

There was a hissing in the silence, and then a rushing, a thundering.

The platform shook, the sun seemed to lose its strength and coldness fell upon the people of the valley as a swirling column of what seemed to be black smoke appeared right there, right between the couple and the cleric's altar, streaming swirls of smoke and darkness, and it became bigger, and the royal court sprang to their feet and there were cries of fear and horror as from the swirling darkness strode a man, all dressed in billowing robes of black, his face a terrible sight.

He strode forward and simply grabbed the princess around the waist; she was stiff with shock and did not fight him, and by the time the prince had recovered his wits and started after the intruder, the black magician had already pulled the princess deep into the swirling darkness and both of them had disappeared.

Then, there was a voice, dark and angry, and it said, "My curse on you and all your generations! May suffering be all that you will ever know from this day hence! In the name of Shakastra, so it will be."

As the voice faded, so did the swirling darkness; it grew smaller and smaller and then it was gone.

But the day was no longer bright; and not soon later, it began to rain on the distraught and weeping queens and courtiers, and on the angry desperate kings and generals as they postured, shouted, blamed and argued; and then thunder and lightning began to flash as those who came this day to be united fell right back into the state they'd been before and fighting then broke out, not just amidst the kings and courts, but everywhere the people of the valley had assembled on this day for celebration; and it was worse and grew more bitter still than ever it had been before.

The princess Harmony opened her eyes to find herself in a most strange place, a most bitter place, a place of dread and misery like she had never known, not even in her dreams.

The land was black and broken; the sky was black and torn grey clouds loomed and twisted. The very air was black as smoke and dense and bitter. The wind was hard and it hissed and clawed at her white dress and at her train of sweetest silks and finest lace.

She found it hard to breathe and hard to move and then she heard the sounds and noises, wailings, screamings, frightful scratchings in the dark, some near, some far, and it was then she knew that she had been transported to a terrifying place and far away from home.

Now any other princess would have cried and shivered, called for help but Harmony was different from other princesses.

It was said about her that she had been born under a blessed star and that the angels had come to visit her as a small child and given her the most unusual gifts of beauty and of wonderment; and as she grew, she laughed at all of that and thought herself to be just like most others who had been reared in beauty and with love, and that the fact that frightened horses calmed at her approach, and wild birds would show no fear and sit by her, and flowers bloomed more richly in her rooms than anywhere was nothing so profound or even special.

There are many girls who are of even temper and who see the good in all and everything around them; but Harmony saw not the good, she simply saw.

She saw and never did she judge; and here, amidst this place of horrors and so far away from home, she saw just as she had always done.

She saw and heard; she saw a creature at her feet, and others would have said that it was hideous, and ugly, and terribly deformed, and evil, but the Princess Harmony just saw a creature and she felt its sadness, its confusion; and just for a moment, this became far more important to her than the many questions as to where she was or what was to become of her, and she bent down and gently touched the creature at her feet, a little touch of recognition and of simple friendliness, attention did she give and the small creature startled and it turned its strange receptors, feeler-eyes upon her in return and it was no longer sad.

The creature crawled and creedled on its way and the princess watched it for a while, and she did never know that just this creature and its kind were lethal, poisonous and feared by all in this dimension, in this place.

With the creature gone, the princess looked around and in the distance, she saw a something that appeared to be a building, a tower so it seemed, with ghostly shadow lights of green appearing now and then.

Now others might have looked upon this tower and they may have cringed and thought that it was most foreboding, ugly and disturbing; but Harmony just saw, and as there was only shards of rock and black-thorned creeping bushes all around, she picked up her enormous wedding dress and started on her way towards it, thinking there may be someone inside who could inform her of what had happened here.

She had only taken a few steps before she was pulled back and brought up sharp; her long train had become ensnared most hopelessly amidst the thorny bushes and she was quite stuck, quite tethered and she turned around and saw and laughed.

Her laughter resonated strangely across and through the broken land and cutting winds; and it was heard by many, big and small; and if the princess had been any other princess, she would have been most fearful now as in response, there was much howling, screeching, and it seemed to come now closer, moving in on where she was engaged in cutting at the train with a sharp edged stone she picked up from the ground.

The gentle and expensive fabric was no match for the diamond sharp edged hardness of the glassy black stone shard and she cut herself loose in no time. Leaving the long white train caught in the bushes behind her, a white pathway in an all black land, she picked up her skirts once more and carefully picked her way in her silk white shoes that were not suited to the harshness of the ground, heading towards the tower and its green lights in the distance.

From far above, from where the howling screams did seem to come, if you were like a huge winged demon dragon flying over this blackened landscape, you would see the princess dressed in white and tiny, shining out just like a lighthouse in a sea of nightblack waves, moving towards the tower, quite a distance, far away and marked out as other and available to all the residents of this unfortunate realm.

And if you were the princess and you looked up into the torn and thundery sky with boiling clouds of lead and pitch black smoke, you would see a huge winged demon dragon circling you, and roaring its screams, and you would know that it had seen you and it was coming closer.

Now many other princesses would have screeched and started to run; but this one simply saw, and she saw the demon dragon, and she also saw that there was no way to outrun it; there was no way to fight it, and in fact, there was not much that she could do but simply turn around and stand and wait.

The dragon circled her; huge it was, with giant leathery wings that were torn here and there; and scaly skin of black, encrusted with welts and scars; old it was, and its eyes were red and fierce fires were burning within.

Harmony stood and turned below and watched its flight; she felt its hunger and its resolution, but also its confusion for this dragon had not seen the likes of her before and it was wary that the princess might conceal a weapon, or that her body might contain a poison, or that her very presence was a trap.

And yet, the dragon circled closer, drawn to the unusual creature white before it and then land it did, with a swirling rushing of its great wings that churned the smoky air, raised clouds of dust and made the princess cover up her eyes.

When she could see again, the head of the dragon was right in front of her and she was looking straight into its fiery eyes; and what she saw was most mysterious to her for she was young, and this dragon was very, very old; it had seen and lived so many things that Harmony had no conception of and she was fascinated as she touched the being, and the purpose of the dragon.

The dragon, old although it was, was most perplexed; not ever had it met or seen a one that would not either be its ready prey and therefore, most afraid; or who would be an enemy to which the dragon would fall prey instead — this creature here before him was entirely other than what it had ever known and so it was that the dragon too became quite fascinated with the girl and both quite simply stood in an embrace of deep attention, each locked upon the other with their eyes and ears and all the other senses they possessed.

What might have happened next, we'll never know; for from the distance, there was then a sound, a sound of strange horns, wailing, rising up and when the dragon heard the sound, it snapped its big and ancient head right up into the air, a movement that was fast and hard and shocked the princess into stepping back.

"What is that?" she asked aloud, and the dragon turned at the sound of her voice and for one moment, it was there again with her and in her mind it was as though she heard a whisper or a sound that gave her knowing that the slayers were approaching and that there was now, no safety to be expected any longer.

This lasted only for a heartbeat and then, the dragon turned away and swiftly, and with giant beating of its leathery wings began to draw away and to ascend, fast, faster still, and higher, until it was quite lost within the darkened boiling sky and once again, the princess found herself alone.

And yet, the sound of wailing, drifting horns of hunt came closer, and with that, the feeling Harmony had learned when she had listened to the dragon, a deep sense of loathing and foreboding and it made her look around for shelter.

The princess saw some greater of the sharp black rocks that covered everything upon this plane, and made her way towards them even as the sounds grew louder at her back, and so she hid behind the rocks and curled herself up tight and pulled her wedding skirts in tightly all around her, and she lay and waited then with beating heart as first, she heard more sounds of movements, and then voices, until they were so close that she could feel them too.

The sound of feet, of heavy hooves, and harsh, loud voices; other sounds of hissing and of heckling, and soon enough, the princess was discovered by a creature that seemed large and like a snake, but it had legs and wore a collar; it had crept across the rocks and stared at her with alien eyes and then gave voice to tell its masters she was there; and soon enough, there were the slayers, tall and fierce, like men yet not like men at all and dressed in metal, silver dull, their skins seemed metal too and they wore bones and shards of stones deep woven in their hair.

Tall lances did they carry; and many knives of great length; and the princess Harmony was dragged from her hiding place by two of them and she was held between them and presented to the leader who looked more ferocious still than all the rest.

Now any other princess would have been entirely terrified; but Harmony was calm and clear, and she was quite aware that she had hidden not because of what she thought herself, but what the dragon had been telling her when they were so connected, and the feelings of dislike and hatred did not come from her, but came from there instead; and so she faced the leader of the slayers fair and square, and looked into his eyes that seemed as cold and hard as all the rocks and shards upon the plane, or harder still, and sought to know him, as she did, and sought to see and understand.

The leader spoke; it was a harsh and hissing tone, the words were not in any tongue that Harmony had heard or learned before, so when he stopped, she answered in her own words, "I can't understand you, I am from far away."

Her voice was clear, it was bright and steady and at its sound, the leader, all the other slayers and even their tracking beasts cocked their heads and were more curious still.

The leader reached out a great gloved hand, which seemed to be like claws, encased in metal as it was and lightly touched with it the princess, touched her hair and touched her skin, a strange sensation, cold and vibrant; Harmony did not resist, she neither struggled nor did she cry, but stood and let the leader learn from this connection more about her, and her kind.

Then, the leader turned and shouted orders; Harmony was lifted and was placed upon a great black animal that seemed just like a dragon, but bereft of wings; the other slayers mounted up as well and soon they all turned and at speed, and faster still across the violent landscape, all the hunt was rushing once more, on their way.

And so it was that Princess Harmony arrived some hours later at the fortress of the slayers.

It was made from the same stone that was scattered everywhere, assembled into crooked walls; it was a part of all this land and seemed to have been grown right from the stone strewn planes. The fortress wasn't very high and there were no windows, no gardens, no decorations of any kind; indeed, you would not know that it was there until you were near right upon it.

There were many guards and doors that were more like the entrance to a cave than doors would be in Harmony's own world; and once the hunt had entered there, and many, many slayers had replaced the huge and stony doors behind them, they were then inside and there were fires, torches, burning strangely pale and with a flint of purple, alien flames that once again reminded Harmony that she was very far from home, indeed.

She was taken then by two guards and the leader even deeper, deep inside the fortress and there now where more of these strange metallic people, and now, there were children and women too, and even though it was a strange place, Harmony did recognise that they were heading for a kind of palace, or the buildings where the rulers of these people would reside.

Deep underground, she was taken; and everywhere, the slayer people stared and hissed and whispered to themselves, and it was warm, and hotter as they went, and Harmony got tired from the walking, but at last they did arrive at a place that was other than the rest of all the fortress.

Here, the walls were clear and sweeping; black reflective, the stone unbroken and it had been shaped to make what seemed to be a palace, and before it lay a still black lake, reflecting back upon the walls and back upon itself, and there was a walkway from the same black glassy stone but smooth it was, and Harmony knew that the rulers were inside that building, deep and deeply underground.

The leader and the guards stood aside and Harmony stepped forward upon the smooth black walkway. She could see herself reflected clearly in the shiny black material of the palace walls, in the distance; and she could see her reflection in the walkway, and also, in the pool that lay either side and she understood that all of this was made of the same material, yet some was hard, and some was liquid.

She began to walk forward on the mirror smooth walkway and toward the great doors and she could see herself in her dishevelled hair, and the wedding dress all torn and ragged, smeared with dust and ash, and it was as though she was walking into herself as she got closer, and closer still.

When she was so close that she might have reached and touched the mirror black doors of the palace, the two wings opened wide and inside, and Harmony took a deep breath and stepped across the threshold and into a big sweeping room with many columns and with many slow, long steps that rose towards a platform upon which and high above, it seemed that some one or some thing was resting, lying down.

It was completely silent; not a sound for Harmony to hear, just her own breath and the rustling of the wedding dress as she began to step up on the first step and to walk along; between the black reflective columns there burned torches, alternating flames of green and purple, reflecting back upon themselves and on the image of the princess who kept moving forward in the silence, forward and then up as one long slow step after the next began to raise her higher as she went, and higher still, until at last she then could see the platform and the being who was resting there.

Now many other, any other princess might have seen a perfect shape of silver bright, and they might well have thought that it appeared much like a dragon, only smaller and the size of just a single man or woman, wearing no clothes at all, only their skin which seemed to be like tiny feathers, smooth and silky; but it was this day and in this place that Harmony saw more, and when she did, she came to understand that not only did she see, she had always seen far more than others who did also think that they could see.

For Harmony did see as well as this exquisite creature made of flowing silver light another shape that occupied the same space as the silver dragon; and it was a woman, stately, like a queen, and yet she too did not wear any clothes, and both were one and yet they weren't quite the same.

Just one more step, and Harmony had now arrived and was upon the level where the platform stood no more than half a man in height, and now she hesitated for she did not want to break this creature's dreams or interfere with it, she was content to stand and watch with awe and see that these things which she saw might still not be the whole truth of that being, that there might be more for her to see, and know, and so she stood and gave the being all her rapt attention, and all fell away from her, as all she was, was forward movement, deep desire now to know and really understand the truth that so presented now to her.

And it was then that on the platform there was movement; the sleeping being seemed to be awakening, and all its many shapes and forms began to shift and shape as it became aware of Harmony in turn, and finally, there was a knowing and a welcome right inside, and our princess knew that she was being spoken to, although this wasn't speech, nor were there words.

So for a time, the princess and the dragon lady did commune with one another, and they found out so many

things about the state and being of each other; and they
had questions and there was a great deal that was simply
quite incomprehensible to each and one.

The dragon lady was as old as Harmony was young;
and she quite failed to understand why Harmony would
choose to clad herself in dirty rags that stopped her movement and precluded flight; and Harmony in turn quite
failed to understand what life would be if one had many
forms and shapes and all of those would live quite different lives and all at once, at that — but still, they talked
and came to grow quite fond of one another and enjoyed
themselves, so much in fact, that it was that Harmony
grew faint with hunger and with thirst, with tiredness.

The dragon lady called and servants came, dressed in
flowing robes and quite unlike the harsh metallic slayer
people of the fortress but not unlike them in their shapes
and aspects of their skin and limbs; Harmony was led
to rooms within the palace where she was given strange
fruit and wine, a pool for her to bathe in, and new clothes
of silken smoothness that were like a second skin, as silver pale as she herself was beautiful, and then she too
was led to platform that was warm and soft, and here
she curled up in great comfort and in satisfaction, and
she fell asleep.

She dreamed, and in her dreams she walked and
talked once more with the dragon lady and she learned of
many things; and it was here that she expressed a wish
that she might be allowed to go back home, to her family
and her prince, who were awaiting her.

But the dragon lady didn't know how such a thing
would be achieved; for she and all her kind did not travel
with their bodies, but instead, had many bodies and in

different places, and it was their mind's awareness that would travel here and there, between the worlds. It was a strange concept to the dragon lady to be travelling and taking any body on the journey, and when she enquired how the princess had arrived, and heard the tale of the ferocious man who dressed in black and spoke in the name of Shakastra who had brought the princess here, the dragon lady knew at once and both agreed that Harmony should go and find this wizard, and procure her means of home return from him at once.

And so it was that when the princess Harmony awoke upon her cosy platform from her sleep, it was already all arranged; and she was clad in shining robes and warming cloak of finest silver, and boots that snuggled round her feet and that were stronger than the hardest leather, yet more soft than silken stockings, and a great dragon was brought for her, and an escort of many slayers to safe guard her on her journey across the land, to the tower Harmony had seen, and where the dragon lady knew the alien wizard did reside.

And just before she left the palace, the dragon lady rose in body from her platform, and she seemed to flow down all the stairs and went to Harmony, and gave her a necklace with a beautiful pendant, luminescent pearly white and shimmering, shaped like a tear, and she told Harmony that if she wanted to speak, or dream with her, this magic pendant would create a bridge, no matter where, no matter when, to bring them both together once again.

Harmony was deeply moved both by the beauty and the kindness of the ancient dragon lady and she took the gift; she expressed her sorrow that she had nothing to give in return, or to repay the dragon lady for her kindness and her friendship.

But the dragon lady wove a movement and it spoke and said that to have met one such as Harmony was gift enough and something well worth waiting for and counting as a great, great prize.

Sitting high in comfort on her stately mount, and with a hundred slayers front, and a hundred further at her back, and with the dragon lady sending wishes of blessing and farewell, the princess Harmony made her way from the palace, out into and through the underground fortress, and out into the darkening planes, to begin her journey that would lead her to Shakastra.

When first the princess Harmony had seen Shakastra's tower from the distance, with eerie green lights ghosting here and there, she had a sense of that it was in ill repair. Now, and much closer up, and getting closer, mounted on a being like a dragon but bereft of wings and clad in luminescent robes of flowing silver white, Harmony could see that it was melting and disintegrating.

What once had been a very stately structure, soaring high and powerfully, and composed of many towers all together was no better than a ruin.

Great gashes had been raked into the sides and walls, exposing crumbling stone much like a wound; the outside layers which had once been smooth and shiny had been all but worn away by time and by attack as well, it seemed. The windows of this ancient ruin were all broken; in some, shards did still remain and all the rest lay black and empty — just apart from two or three, right at the very top, from which the greenish light was flickering.

It was cold now and the winds were higher, more bitter still and if it had not been for the dragon lady's wondrous gifts of clothing, cape and shoes the princess would have frozen soon enough; but as it was, the clothing warmed her body, and the magic jewel warmed her heart, and that, together with the knowledge that inside this tower was a one who might procure her passage back to her own home, the valley green and far away, gave Harmony both strength and spirit; and as well, she was now keenly fascinated to meet up with the magician and to ask him why he had abducted her.

The slayers took her right up to the base of the great ancient tower complex, where there was an enormous doorway leading into pitch black dark, with doors long gone and broken down and into long ago; but they would go no further then, and so it was the princess all alone, save for a purple fire torch, who walked into the ancient silence.

Out of the wind, and once inside, it was indeed most quiet.

Harmony stood in a huge circular entrance hall, with crumbling walls and not a trace of furniture or decoration left, with fallen masonry strewn across the floor, and raised her purple fire torch up high to see the stairs that spiralled up and up into the darkness up above.

These stairs were too in ill repair and made from stone, that black and glassy stone that everything was made of in this broken night dimension; but they did swoop still, and it was as well the truth that Harmony could only go now forward, up, there was no turning back and really, nothing else left now to do.

And so the princess Harmony began the long and slow ascent, and picked her way with care across the dusty, stone strewn stairs, and she walked slowly but with will for it was such a long way up, and such a climb, and she did thank in mind the dragon lady for the chance of rest and for her food and friendliness, and as she climbed from stair to stair, and wound her way up higher and still higher in the darkness, with her purple torch that made a small but welcome island made of light around her, it was as though the dragon lady was still with her, and sending her support, and courage on her task.

She climbed for what did seem as though forever; and every so often, Harmony would simply stop and rest a while, but not for long; and she did also keep her eyes ahead and up, for if she should look back or down, not only would she see the stairs receding into pitch black gloom but also the sheer drop into the empty centre of the tower and although the princess Harmony was brave, that was not something she did like to contemplate for any length of time.

But finally she did arrive, and finally, she did emerge onto a platform, and the endless stairs had ended, and there was a doorway and there was the green light that had first alerted her to find this place, to come here and to ask for help.

She stepped into the doorway and she followed to the green light shining; and then she found a large apartment, round and clearly high, high up in this tower, and it had windows all around, and some were broken and they had been boarded up with blackened planks, and some were still intact and kept the wind of night at bay; and there was ancient furniture, all brittle and already near collapse, and there was a kind of bed, and on this bed, there lay a man.

This was indeed a man as Harmony found out, when she came carefully a little closer. He was of her father's age but thinner, paler and his hair was white; he looked most frail and quite forsaken, lying there beneath the remnants of old rags and tapestries he had assembled to keep out the cold that seeped from every stone, and every crack, and even seemed to fall right from the roof itself.

The green light she had seen came from a strange and flickering fire that was sitting in the middle of the room, half in mid air and gave no heat, no warmth; but it did give some light and also, it did battle with the purple torch the princess was still holding, causing a most strange sensation, making it most difficult to see; so Harmony put down the torch a way away, and then went closer to the sleeping man.

She called him softly, and when he did not seem to hear, she touched him on the shoulder; and it was then she saw that he was ill and not just sleeping; and not just ill, but very ill and likely close to death.

There was no water she could offer him; no food. There was no pail or stove to cook a broth, if even Harmony had known how this was done, and she did not; there were no medicines, just nothing that could be of help here and so this was now the first time that the princess felt as though she lost her heart and a great darkness weighed upon her; she sat down next to the man, and drew her warming cloak around her far more tightly, and just looked down at him and hoped to see a something, feel a something, sense a something that could help her here to find some plan of action, something she could do, but nothing came to her this night, and this light, and at this time, and so she sat until she must have lain down right beside him, and she fell asleep, and then asleep more deeply still, and then she dreamed...

In dreams, it is the case that usually you never know that you are dreaming; and when you awake within the dream, the dream will end; and so it was at first for Harmony who too had failed to notice that she fell asleep, and in her dream it was all real and she was running through the green and pleasant meadows just beyond the formal palace gardens of her home; she was running fast and wearing her wedding dress with its long train that made it hard to run, but run she did and she saw a man and thought it was her Arran, was her prince.

He stood in the meadow grass surrounded by flowers, and he was young and beautiful, but when she came closer, there was something not quite right about him or not quite as though she did remember right.

His clothes were right; a state uniform of midnight blue, unbuttoned though it was, with much gold trimming, and a brightwhite shirt beneath, and matching trousers, matching boots.

His hair was right, his eyes were right, his size was right and yet his presence was so different that Harmony slowed down and stopped before she threw herself into his arms, and tried to see and seek to know this difference.

He was a stranger to her but he looked at her and smiled and said, "Are you late for your wedding?"

Harmony looked down upon herself, at her dress and fine white gloves and was confused again — who was this man, and why was she thus dressed and running in a meadow?

"I think I'm lost," she said to the man who seemed familiar and yet was a total stranger to her, and the man who looked like Arran smiled again and nodded and he said, "I think I'm lost as well. I don't know what I'm doing here."

Harmony listened to the sound of his voice, his way of speaking and she had the strangest notion of remembrance, of a far away familiarity with a something she could neither trace nor frame and then the man said to her, "That's a beautiful jewel you are wearing, I've never seen anything quite like it," and she looked down at herself again and saw a brightwhite tear-shaped pendant on her own chest, flashing high and hard beneath the early summer sun and it was then that Harmony awoke within the dream, and she remembered, but she also fought to stay within the dream because she knew this man must be the old one who was sleeping sick beneath the rags, who couldn't talk for real and who might be the only one who knew just how to get them home.

So slowly and most carefully, the princess said, "My name is Harmony. Are you Shakastra?"

The handsome man looked puzzled and he shook his head, "No, dear lady," he said in response, "my name is Arran. Who is this Shakastra that you seek?"

And now, the princess Harmony was most confused, for Arran was the name of her own bridegroom, a name of princess and of kings a long time in the valley, and it occurred to her that in this dream she should be speaking to an ancestor of Arran's, someone from a time back when, and this was hard to tell for flowers bloom the same no matter how the years are passing, and that blue uniform he wore was just the same as it had been for centuries and passed along the generations.

"What do you know of dragons, and of towers?" These words just came to Harmony, she knew not how or where or why but spoke them, and it was as though she spoke the words of magic for the man stepped back in shock, and brought his hands up to his face and looked upon them, looked down upon himself and she could see that he was now awakening as well, for he became translucent and as though he was a ghost that faded in the sunlit dream, and she called to him to steady him and stay with her and take this chance to talk and to resolve what might be done about their situations.

She called Shakastra, but that did not help and more and more he faded; but when she called him Arran, strange for her as Arran was another altogether, it was that he too woke within the dream and came to be more real, and realer still, until they both were once again together, right here on this most beautiful of days, right here within this sunny meadow, and both knew just who and why they were, why they were here.

The man sat down upon the grass and Harmony did sit beside him; and there he told her of his life and how he had displeased his brother who had been the king; displeased him such that in his fury, the king had declared him invisible to all, and laid a bane of death upon each and every person who would give him shelter, a word or even one single look.

He told her of his hardship, how he had been forced to steal from fields to stay alive, and how he'd found the tower, far away from everyone and in the mountains, where he lived all by himself for many years, and how his anger and resentment grew at his ill treatment; and how after years of sending letter after letter, asking for his brother's mercy he had turned away and then instead began to hate his brother, first the king, and then the court, and he had ended up with hating everyone in the entire kingdom.

And finally, he told her of the wedding day and how he swore that he would bring them suffering that lasted all their generations, how he had taken the sweet bride and left her all alone to die in a demonic place at the far reaches of the universe.

But when he did return, he found that he had been well recognised; and not just the king and all his troops but also all the people in the valley had made their way to his old tower and had torn it all to pieces, screaming for Shakastra's blood.

In haste, he fled; in haste, he took the first available doorway and in his haste, he landed at the last place he had been — the same dimension where he had marooned the princess.

Now, with his home tower having been entirely destroyed and totally erased, there was no going back — the doorway had gone, the mirror tower to the other side which one would need to travel there between was now no longer there, and he could not return himself, and nor could princess Harmony.

All these things he told her as they sat most comfortably in their mutual dream, and it was there as well that he apologised to her and took her hand and kissed it, and he said that he would gladly die to put the wrongs he did to rights, if only this would help to take her back, for it was not her fault and he was wrong to have abducted her, to let his anger grow to be a monster that could then no longer be controlled and create all these events that now, he was quite powerless to change at all.

Harmony sat and looked and listened and she was most sad, and more for him and for his wasted life than for herself, but she was young and never given to give up; and so she said, "Now Arran, or Shakastra, you are a magician. You did bring us here. You know of magical things — there must be something we can do. If we cannot return to home as yet, perhaps there's something else — to heal you, make you better so that there is time for us to make a better plan."

"I don't really have much magic," Arran sighed. "What once I knew was all a lot of tricks — just using old machines and magic items that were left from times before. And now, without those items, and without the books, I have no tricks and I can't know what might still save us here."

So both then sighed and sat and drifted with their own thoughts; and as they did, the dreamtime sun above did move through time and then there came a time when once again, it struck the jewel on the silver chain, and Harmony did see and she exclaimed, "The dragon lady! She is there, and she will bring you aid and comfort. She has food and water, warmth and wisdom, I will try to take you there in body, so you'll be restored, and perhaps if we all work together, we can find a way."

Arran sighed and said, "You should return there by yourself and leave me here to die. I don't deserve much better, and I am of little help — you go and save yourself, sweet princess, and I wish you luck, for what it's worth."

And that was when the dreaming ended and the princess woke to find herself in that most horrid freezing crumbling tower with the old man who was near to death, and a sense of dread and desperation on her heart.

She could not carry him for he had been a tall man in his youth; and yet she could not leave him here for he would never be alive on her return if she would walk the distance to the slayer's fortress, if she could find it even out within that sea of broken stones and shards where every one direction looked the same as all the others.

But what else was there to do?

The princess rose and went to the window arches, tried to see but could not see for all the windows they were old and blind and dusty, smeared with ash, and so she looked around and then she found another door, a walkway out into the cold dark night that never seemed to end, and she did shudder but she thought to look around at least, at least lay a direction, and at least have tried to reach the fortress for she could not be here and do nothing.

So the princess opened the last door in the tower room, and rushing, bitter wind did enter and it nearly swept her off her feet, but still, she bravely faced it and went right into it, climbed the narrow winding steps and then emerged upon a walkway, high and higher still above the broken land.

All around her lay the night, a never ending night of howling storms and boiling clouds, swirling dust and darkness, cold and harsh it was, and endless; whichever direction Harmony turned in, the view was always the same — there was nothing out there in those darkened lands but broken stone, an ocean where nothing could nourish, nothing could grow.

And it was here that for the first time since she had arrived, Harmony felt a terrible sadness, and a despair; she felt so small, so alone, and so completely helpless as she had never felt before; and also for the first time, the thought that she might have to suffer here until she died came to her, and that was not the kind of thought this princess had ever known before.

Harmony didn't know what to do.

Her life had been so blessed; so easy. She had always walked in lightness and with love and flowering of so much wealth and true abundance all around, in every way; whatever challenges there might have been did not prepare her for this night, for her own feelings, and she put her hands before her eyes, and bowed her head, and then she cried.

And as she cried, her tears fell, hot and rich; and they fell on her chest, and one perfect drop fell straight onto the brightwhite jewel of the dragon lady.

When Harmony's tear touched the mirror smooth surface of the jewel, a strange but wonderful transformation began; at first, the princess did not notice that the jewel shone more brightly, and more brightly still but soon she saw, and soon she gasped and stepped right back as on her chest, a star was flaring like a new born sun, and bright and brighter still the light did flare, so bright that Harmony could now no longer look at it and had to close her eyes again, but even through her closed lids, the brightness rose, and rose again and more, and more, and wider and wider was the radiance and brightness, casting forward, out, into an ever widening circle, yet there was no heat, there was no pain and Harmony just knew that something most extraordinary was occurring here, and that it wasn't meant to do her harm, but that indeed, this might have come to help her in her darkest hour.

The radiance got brighter still, and brighter still and then it was as though although her eyes were tightly shut, another kind of eyes were opening who knew to see this kind of light, who had been waiting for this light to now reveal before and all around a different existence as Harmony began to breathe again and stood in awe and reverence, as with her other eyes she saw that what she thought had been just broken rocks and shard were nothing of the kind; that there, below and all around lay a most wonderful of landscapes, rich with life and dancing with the colours and existence, that there was moisture, and nourishment, and that the beings there were beautiful and perfect, that they had most wondrous ways of being and of doing, and the sky was filled with living, dancing, singing light and it was here that Harmony began to understand the what this land was impossible to see with eyes that were so used to other kinds of land, to other skies; and they had failed to understand and comprehend at all just where she was, and what was happening here.

The princess stood upon a mighty tower, and it wasn't old, nor was it ruined in the slightest way; it was fantastic and entirely built of light, alive and humming, knowing and supportive of everyone who entered there. Around her, wind beings were dancing and telling her of their existence, of their ways; and high up in the glorious symphonic skies, she could see dragons, golden, beautiful and absolutely perfect.

Harmony turned, and wherever she placed her gaze, there was more wonder, more perfection still; and she saw the fortress of what she thought were slayers, but she saw them as they truly were now, and they were beautiful, and so were their lands, their great town and most of all, the radiant palace of the dragon lady, who became aware — although it was so far away — of Harmony's wide gaze and her attention and in turn, she rose and looked around, and both could see each other just as clearly as if they were in the same room, face to face.

There came a knowing and a smiling from the dragon lady, for she had been trying to teach Harmony to see the truth of all this land and this dimension all along but had not found a way beyond the giving of the jewel, and the hope that it might do the trick, become the catalyst, and it had been, indeed, and Harmony did bow her head and send a smile of deepest, heartfelt gratitude; her smile became a prayer, then a blessing and it flew from her like silken banners, and it reached the dragon lady and enveloped her, and stroked her, flowed all about her and the Princess Harmony was joyous, radiant and free, and never more than she had been this day of revelations.

Harmony gazed and touched the land, the beings with her smile; and all did love her in return; the ancient dragons in the skies above made her a song, and sang it in her honour, and Harmony stood on the soaring tower and her voice joined theirs, her arms spread awide, and this day was, indeed a blessing for the widest of unfoldments, and the song and time did ripple right across the levels and the layers, resonating all and bringing dreams of glorious colours, hushing touch of smiling winds and radiance to beings far and further still, above, below, and everywhere.

And it was then that Harmony did turn her gaze to find the sleeping man within the tower, and when she touched him with her gentle power, he too did awaken, and he too was not a starving, bitter, evil, dying man at all, but a great being of immense and awesome beauty, and so it was that Arran who had once been known as the magician Shakastra awoke into the radiance, and understood, and was healed of all things, and was raised, and also then accepted and most welcomed to the web of all that did exist in this enchanted place.

So they celebrated for a long time, took the nourishment and the enchantment and they used it both to raise themselves and to restore themselves in every way, and they did learn so many things, and they did grow, and they did change, and yes they knew that they were changing.

There came a time when both could open now their eyes of real and here and yet, the other eyes remained wide open too, and that then brought a merger and Harmony and Arran came together, held hands and simply traced the vortex patterns that had brought them here; there was no need for old machines or even towers for it is indeed quite easy to be travelling amongst the manifold dimensions, if your eyes are open and you can perceive the gateways and the portals that exist between the worlds.

On a blue, blue early summer's day, when the young sun was bright and gold high in the sky, and the valley was green and luscious, many flowers in the meadows and the fields and orchards showing all the bountiful abundance that was soon to come our way, the princess Harmony and prince Arran the elder simply appeared exactly where they'd vanished, one year to the day and to the moment.

There was no wedding platform anymore; and there was no-one now around; and the land did show the signs of war and desperation; but when they arrived, so did the light that they could see and that was now a part of everything that they would touch.

Most practically, and most together they did call a meeting of the warring kingdoms; and there wasn't anyone at all could stand up against their light and will combined; and peace was declared immediately, between the families and inside the families as well.

Harmony did marry her young prince in the end; she thus became the queen and helped Arran, who once had been Shakastra the magician start a university of learning about the other worlds, and the building was placed right into the centre of the valley, and construction began as soon as the wedding ceremony had concluded.

In time, the valley became a centre for travellers, explorers and artists from many worlds, from many different planes and it was a most wondrous place to be; and those who didn't know just how to visit there, would visit anyway, and even if it was in dreams.

Story Teller StarFields

In Serein

Lose yourself in the extraordinary In Serein Trilogy — a modern day masterpiece in magical fantasy.

Vampire Solstice

Master Story Teller Starfields takes on the Vampire myth — and you can be guaranteed to find a story here you won't have heard before.

The Magician

Follow Anna as she leaves her old life behind and makes her way to the White Mountains to find the magician.

Project Sanctuary

Imagine a book that contains all stories — and these are YOUR stories! If you are fascinated with story, metaphor, imagination and the boundless creativity of the human mind and spirit, Project Sanctuary will be the best book you have ever owned.

Available From All Good Bookshops
Or Directly From
DragonRising Publishing UK
www.DragonRising.com